F. T Wilson

Surf

A summer pilgrimage

F. T Wilson

Surf
A summer pilgrimage

ISBN/EAN: 9783337289201

Printed in Europe, USA, Canada, Australia, Japan

Cover: Foto ©Andreas Hilbeck / pixelio.de

More available books at **www.hansebooks.com**

A SUMMER PILGRIMAGE.

BY

SAUL WRIGHT.

———

NEW YORK:
FORDS, HOWARD, & HULBERT.

TO

James M. Bailey,

Journalist, Humorist and Sage,

TO WHOSE GENIAL AND INDULGENT FRIENDSHIP

THESE LETTERS

WERE ADDRESSED AND THROUGH WHOSE FLATTERING

ENCOURAGEMENT I AM TEMPTED TO PUBLISH THEM,

This Book

IS RESPECTFULLY DEDICATED BY

THE AUTHOR.

CONTENTS.

AN APOLOGY.

THE letters which form the motive for this book were actually written in cold blood, with premeditated forethought, and addressed to my friend Bailey, of Danbury, Conn., without the slightest expectation of their ever wandering beyond a certain circumscribed orbit. That he has survived the infliction, has encouraged me to intrude them upon that most indulgent community—the American people. Let me plead in extenuation that this is my first offense, with every reasonable expectation of its being the last. If, then, I may hope to be released with a reprimand, it's

SAUL WRIGHT.

WASHINGTON, May 1, 1881.

I.

The Pilgrims.

On Board the "Lady of the Lake,"
Potomac River, August 1, 18—.

When Thucydides suggested the return of our usual summer tramp the other day, I am free to confess the idea did not strike me with its usual force. Perhaps there were reasons for this absence of enthusiasm not altogether inconsistent with the popular idea of a "tramp," and perhaps there were not. I am not going to argue the point. To the individual who has not endured the agonies of an "extra session" of Congress it would be impossible to convey any idea of the supreme blessings of—rest. When one has been obliged for nearly four wretched months to report the goings-out and the comings-in of a few hundred, more or less, of sweltering Congressmen who haven't known their own minds over night, and who have been known to change their firm opinions and convictions twenty-four times within as many consecutive hours ; when one has been forced to listen to the chatter of political magpies who call each other liars, blackguards, and cowards at one moment, and sit down to discuss a jovial lunch of terrapin and *champagne frappé* together the next, the sublime delight accompanying the reaction is altogether too ecstatic to be tampered with. When one—but pshaw! let it be said in a word without further circumlocution, that even a reporter, with no particular soul to save, has rights which even his friends are bound — occasionally — to respect. Hence, I plunge directly into the midst of my narrative by remarking that we are "on the road."

It is possible that the monosyllabic "we" is not altogether explanatory. Yet, how else may I designate four ambitious knights of the quill, who sincerely trust that, should the gods be propitious, they may in time be exalted to that sublime height from whence they may exchange the pencil for the shears and paste-pot, and sway all humanity through a judicious use of the second person plural? In the order, then, of their importance, permit me to introduce the members of this Bohemian expedition to nowhere in particular. First and foremost, my friend Thucydides, an humble *attaché* of the Chicago *Censor*. Now, "Sid" is a tramp of refinement and varied accomplishments; in fact he is a walking encyclopedia of valuable information, of which in my present degree of apprenticeship, I am frequently and gratefully obliged to avail myself. Upon his classic and middle-aged head is piled up the agony of years, through the sinuous mazes of which he has rubbed against the world, and suffered the customary experience of leaving behind him a considerable portion of the cuticle of egotism, and a fair percentage of the ordinary human temper. Unlike the proverbial rolling stone, he has managed to accumulate an inordinate quantity of the moss of experience, while the consequent friction has developed a highly agreeable polish to the tone of his advice.

I am afraid that Sid is somewhat of a cynic, and that his stock of faith in the good intentions of humanity is decidedly diminutive. He is in the habit of taking me into the Congressional galleries of an afternoon, and, pointing out some public man, proceeds to tear in pieces his political character, as a student in anatomy would dissect an interesting subject, and with about the same regard for the feelings of his victim. And what makes the operation particularly aggravating is the unfortunate way he has of following up his attacks of the scalpel of criticism with the abominable lancet of proof.

When I first knew Sid, he had just been legis-

lated out of the army, through one of those annual
assaults that idle Congresses are wont to make on
an institution they know nothing about, and by
which means its casualties are greater in peace
than in war, and had been forced to sheathe his
sword, because of the treasonable offense of being
at the foot of his grade in the regiment.

Sid's prominent characteristic, after some years
of desultory adventure, is personal assurance, a
virtue that among degenerate minds is frequently
styled "cheek," by which is meant that his countenance is one of surpassing loveliness and un-
blushing candor. Learning from sad experience
that the pen is mightier than the sword, and from
personal observation that the pun is vastly more
remunerative than the item of fact, behold our ex-
warrior tickling, for a livelihood, the sensibilities of
civilized men as he once tickled with a saber the
ribs of the untutored savage. If his present calling is less beneficial to humanity, it is, upon the
whole, more intensely poetic.

And speaking of the poetic reminds me of Jack.
Jack, by the way, is a bright and shining satellite
of the New York *Moon.* Like the mild luminary
from which he borrows his effulgence, he shines
for all, yet Jack's luster is not altogether of a reflected quality, but rather a combination of moon-

beams and gas-light; a compound of quaint origi-
nality and a straining after the sensational effect
for which the luminary in question is so univer-
sally noted. I am afraid that Jack does not hesitate to amplify and enlarge upon the exact truth
upon occasion, but in justice to Mr. Longmeter, I
must confess that the said occasions are mostly
professional. The wonderful and preposterous
proportions to which a questionable rumor has
been known to swell under Jack's manipulations is
only exceeded by the refreshing and open-hearted
candor which distinguishes his contradiction of the
whole story in his next dispatch. Jack has a habit
of disclosing the most remarkable and unsuspected phases of character at the most unexpected
moments, and is generally conceded to be a mystery to his friends, and an agreeable study for the
community at large. By the community at large,
I refer more properly to the female community.
Although the most susceptible youth within the
range of my acquaintance, this unbounded suscep-
tibility is always accompanied by the most glaring
instances of fickleness and inconstancy. Hence
Jack is no less popular with the fair sex than
agreeable to his own, for no one would ever think of
being either vexed with or jealous of Jack, in the
absolute certainty that that worthy's mind is of so

uncertain a quantity that both time and patience would thereby be wholly and uselessly wasted.

Yet, strange as it may appear, Jack has a vulnerable point, and stranger still, the point in question is his intense and undisguised admiration for the poetic Muse. To this adorable damsel Jack is always and pathetically constant. The more glaring does this infatuation appear, when it is considered that Jack has the most supreme contempt for any of his fellow-adorers, and the most utter disregard for their passion or identity. He is quite as likely to confound Byron with Bishop Heber, or Dr. Watts with Dr. Holmes, as to quote an impassioned strophe of Swinburne's as an annex to one of Mrs. Sigourney's devotional inspirations.

And that brings me to Dick. Mr. Richard Palette, *Artium Baccalaureus*, whilom representative of the Boston *Cash Book*, at your service. There is nothing uncertain about Dick. He is intense, ardent, earnest, and sufficient. When you catch Dick at a disadvantage you will have to turn out at an uncommonly early hour of the morning. He is as utterly devoid of sentiment as an oyster of philosophy. I don't imagine Dick was ever in love with anything but himself—and art.

If Dick had not been compelled out of dire necessity to become a collector of political fact and scandal for the daily press, I am confident that the world would long since have gone frantic over him as an artist. It is unfortunate that politics and art cannot well be confounded, and still more unfortunate that the attention exacted by the one is apt to interfere with the devotion demanded by the other. Hence, the habit of arresting one's brush just at the moment one has caught a spark of the divine aflatus, in order to follow up the smoke of a political racket in the House, is apt to disarrange one's ideas, and demoralize one's temper. As a consequence, Dick has never been able to complete anything in the line of high art that he has ever commenced. Not but that he has begun enough in the aggregate to have filled the National Gallery to repletion, had they ever advanced beyond the preliminary stage ; but a visit to Dick's apartments would develop the most remarkable collection of initiated efforts ever witnessed. Landscapes outlined in umber ; historical suggestions in charcoal ; portraits in which a pair of liquid blue eyes gaze down in astonishment upon the skeleton of a pink nose ; marines advanced to the stage wherein a fleet of phantom ships are suspended midway between a cadmium sky and a pea-green ocean. One of these days all of these astounding possibilities are to be completed, and burst sud-

denly upon an enthusiastic community, and then—
then indeed I shall be proud of my friend Dick.

And this is all I propose to explain regarding
the *personnelle* of this expedition, excepting that
upon the undersigned devolves the duties of the
scribe, and that Sid will assume, without effort,
the *rôle* of the Pharisee in this faithful report of a
Midsummer Day's Dream. So far as Jack and
Dick are concerned, they will be expected to contribute the sentimental and the picturesque; to
deal with the esthetics and the finer sensibilities of
the tramp, as a counterpoise to the ruder cyni-
cisms of the Pharisee, and the practical dogmatism
of the Scribe.

There are several excellent reasons why the
schedule of our journey is not inserted at this
point. In reading a work of travels, such as this
is to be, it is desirable to know the line over which
one is expected to follow, the sights one is to
see, or at the least the point at which one is expected to arrive. But in the first place, this tramp
is to differ from the ordinary in most respects;
why not in all? As most works of travel outline
the route, this shall not, out of pure obstinacy.

In the second place, there is nothing so desirable
in a romance as the sense of expectation, and no
right-minded reader will calmly turn to the final

page to learn how the thing is coming out, as do females as a class and school-girls as a genus. So we propose to remove this temptation from our readers *nolens volens*, in the conviction that we shall receive their undying gratitude in the end.

In the third place, we are not going to outline our route in this opening chapter, for the reason that we have not the least conceivable idea of what it is ourselves. And, come to think of it, perhaps this should, after all, have been the first reason instead of the third. But as it is not, let the reader select whichever of the three he, she, or they prefer, and thus maintain their independence. If there is anything the average reader abhors, it is to be led by the nose, as it were. Hence, whether we bring up in the vicinity of Greenland's icy mountains or India's coral strands, no one need feel the slightest disappointment or conceive that they have been in any manner deceived. This much I can promise : that if this ship holds together, and from the creaking and straining at this writing, there is nothing certain about it, the morning will find us on the "broad bosom of the Atlantic." At least I wrenched that much from the brain of the captain a moment ago. Those were not his precise words, by the way ; but as he said we'd be "'way down below the mouth of the river," I merely recalled

2

the remains of a limited anatomical education and made my own deductions.

So the scene opens with the expedition fairly under way. "Under weigh" would perhaps be more nautical, but then one is not expected to assume his sea legs while yet in sight of land, and as yet the only marine monster observed has been the aforesaid captain of the boat, whom I would defy the most experienced reporter to interview with impunity. What a successful Congressman that amphibious monster would make, by the way! How he would shut himself up like one of his own binoculars, and box the ears of an opponent as quickly as he would box his own compass. Not that I ever heard of a sea-captain boxing a compass against time; but as that certainly seems the proper thing for a sea-captain to do, I am not going to spoil a comparison for so paltry a thing as an inconsistency. The scenery thus far on the voyage has not been particularly picturesque. We have left Alexandria in the offing, and are steaming away toward Fort Washington. Sid says that it's the fog that Alexandria is left in; but "offing" sounds better, and what's the good of being at sea if one is not to make use of the few nautical phrases in his vocabulary? There may be something slightly anomalous in the fact of a tramp traveling by steamboat; but when one considers that the pecuniary consideration demanded in exchange for a voyage between Washington and Norfolk and return—a matter of some five hundred miles, more or less—is the beggarly pittance of one hundred and fifty cents, the anomaly is lost, and the joke comes in, you see, with telling effect.

[*Item:* This is not an advertisement for the steamboat company, as future unhappy voyagers between the points in question will learn to their sorrow, when the rival lines have exhausted their surplus funds, or compromised the matter, which will be one and the same thing, so far as the public are concerned.]

As a consequence, the boat is crowded, crammed, overflowing. About one per cent of the crowd are going to Norfolk for legitimate purposes; say ten per cent for pleasure, and the balance for no other reason under the heavens than because they are carried for one dollar and a half. They are as much interested in the trip as though they were riding a block or so in the horse-cars; the trip is, in fact, attended by every imaginable discomfort conse-quent upon the superiority of numbers over accom-modations; the majority will be wretchedly sea-sick, home-sick, and heart-sick before morning, and will wish themselves and the boat at the bottom of the

Potomac a thousand times before daylight; but the recollection of that paltry dollar will be a surcease of all sorrow and a recompense for every misery.

We are passing a charming section of woodland, through the openings of which peep a delightful mansion, whose high-columned portico and dainty cupola supply the motive to what is really an exquisite picture. I inquire of Sid the name of the place, and twenty voices, male, female, and neuter, hasten to respond, "*Mount Vernon.*"

"Ah!" said I, "doubtless the seat of some wealthy Virginian Congressman, perhaps. Or, possibly, the home of some gentleman of reputation."

"Mount Vernon?" says Sid; "the name sounds familiar. But I don't see any mountain."

"Why," shout the twenty voices, "Mount Vernon is the home of Washington. It contains the tomb of the Father of his Country. It is—"

"But, hold on a moment," says Sid; "in other words go slow, and one at a time, if you please. Who is Washington, and what does he want of a tomb? You see we are strangers in this vale of tears, and particularly anxious to acquire knowledge. Is this Mr. Washington one of your public men?"

Here the most of the twenty turn up their noses in disgust, several snicker, and the balance stare at

the wretch as though they would prefer to demol-
ish him. Sid's impassive countenance, however,
dispels all doubts that may have arisen regarding
his being, possibly, a humorist in disguise, and several of the faces, mostly feminine, take on a look of
pity for his ignorance and charity for his unconscious crime. And one benevolent old party, with
a peculiarly sympathetic countenance, goes over to
Sid, and places his broad palm on his knee, with
the remark:

"General Washington, sir, was the greatest man,
beyond all question, who ever lived. When the
American colonies, sir, rose in rebellion—"

"Ah, yes, I see," interrupted Sid, with an im-
pressive wave of his hand; "a Confederate Briga-
dier."

"No, sir! no, sir! this was one hundred years
ago. When the American colonies rose in rebellion
against the mother-country, Washington placed
himself at their head and led them to victory.
He—"

"Ah, yes—now I see why he needs a tomb. A
most commendable precaution, I should say; but
—but—I beg your pardon—but perhaps he is no
longer living?"

"Washington died, sir, on the fourteenth day of
December, seventeen hundred and ninety-nine; but

he lives, my dear sir—he lives in the hearts of his countrymen."

"Indeed! striking coincidence—happy sentiment. I infer, then, that the late Mr. Washington was an American."

"The greatest of all Americans. We honor and love and revere his memory. There is nothing, sir, that America would not do to honor the memory of Washington. We have named our capital city for him, and there is scarcely a state in the Union that has not counties and towns and villages that bear his name. Monuments, statues, squares, and parks perpetuate his fame from one end of the land to the other."

"Indeed! Now I think of it, I did observe, while in Washington, a huge white chimney that reminded me of a grain elevator, set down in the midst of a swamp, that they told me was the Washington Monument. And some flannel drawers and an undershirt or two were shown in a glass case at the Patent Office, and labeled 'Washington's Clothes.' I am glad you mentioned it. What can there be, my venerable friend, more sublime in life than these touching examples of a nation's gratitude. What—"

"And this," said the benevolent old party, hastily interrupting, as he pointed to a dilapidated mansion cosily embowered in a most charming grove on the left bank—"this is Marshall Hall."

"Indeed!" responds Sid, as he sights the sylvan picture through his eyeglasses—"and was Mr. Hall another of your Revolutionary fathers?"

"Mr. Marshall, sir, Mr. John Marshall, a Maryland gentleman of great wealth, and the intimate friend of Washington. You will observe the two estates front each other on opposite banks of the river. The hall was a fine structure in its day, sir, but with the fortunes of the family, has run sadly to decay."

"Did—did this Mr. Marshall—did he leave any monuments and small-clothes?"

"And this quiet little group of trees at the end of the little pier on your right," goes on the b. o. p., utterly oblivious of Sid's inquiry, "is Mount Vernon Springs. The springs, however, are about one mile to the west, and—"

"How charming—pardon me!—how charming is the nomenclature of your river estates. The place above, you call Mount Vernon, because there is no mountain within, I believe, a hundred and fifty miles, and this you call the Springs, for the excellent reason that the nearest spring is a mile distant. Now—"

But whether a suspicion of the truth was begin-

ning to penetrate the brain of the benevolent old
party, or whether he recalled a forgotten engagement at the other end of the boat, may never be
known. He had disappeared, and never returned
to apologize or explain, and with him had disappeared our late audience, leaving us alone, in the
most comfortable part of the boat, to our own devices. But from the suspicious manner with which
we are gazed upon, and pointed at, at safe dis-
tances, by our fellow voyagers, I am convinced
that the report of the aforesaid b. o. p. has not
been altogether flattering.

"Saul," remarks my inseparable as he disposes
his long figure at full length on the bench, and
assumes the most insufferable air of intense satis-
faction with himself and the world, "sit a little
more to the windward, if you please—I find these
breezes a trifle unpleasant on my shoulders—and
hand me one of those Partagas that I saw you pur-
chasing an hour ago; borrow a light for me from
that gentleman yonder, and keep perfectly quiet,
with a strict avoidance of all comments, and I will
give you the benefit of a few morsels of wisdom
that I find I can spare from the bountiful store of
my experience."

Now, as I find nothing of importance transpiring
among the crowd of pleasure-seekers about us ; the

scenery through which we are slowly steaming, while fresh and delightfully verdant, is wretchedly monotonous, and nothing beyond the historical memories of the stream over which we are gliding to make the hour other than commonplace and dull; as Jack and Dick are flirting on the after-deck—in short, as all is quiet on the Potomac, and my cigar is tolerable, I presume I may as well listen to Sid's dreary twaddle as undergo any other penance that occurs to me, so I accept the inevitable with due humility.

"Now then," says Sid, "you will observe that in order to obtain absolute comfort in travel, the first essential for the traveler is perfect and complete stupidity. Your knowing traveler is always burdened with his own conceit, and weighed down by the incubus of his own wisdom. I have always looked upon the human sponge as the most unhappy member of the animal kingdom. He absorbs everything that surrounds him, and being over-floated with wisdom, extends a perpetual invitation for some one to squeeze him. Now that venerable old guide-book doubtless meant well, but he could no more have permitted so brilliant an opportunity to impart wisdom to a stranger to slip him than he could have avoided soaring on the Washington question. It was half his enjoyment of the trip.

It has lightened his heart equal to a dose of seltzer, and he really didn't mind my chaffing him one bit. He put it all down to my ignorance, you know, as a compliment to his own superior culture. On the other hand, you see we are now left in undisputed possession of the most cosily sheltered part of the boat. We are savages, *ignorami*, idiots who, never having heard of these local gods, are beyond the pale of good society. Hence we are left severely to ourselves, while the better herd are packed together yonder on the after-deck, like so many educated sardines.

"There are four rules, my dear fellow, that govern the successful tourist in his peregrinations up and down the earth, and which enable him to endure and positively enjoy them. In the first place he knows nothing, and is never surprised at anything he sees or hears. He thus avoids the society of those superficial souls who, knowing a little of everything, are fond of airing their wisdom at his expense.

"Second. He has no idea where he came from nor where he is going, and hasn't the slightest suspicion what place he will visit *en route*. His stock of knowledge on these points for the benefit of such of his fellow-travelers as are overburdened with curiosity is therefore decidedly limited.

"Third. He has no curiosity. He don't care a picayune whether it is going to rain this evening or shine to-morrow ; don't care how far it is to the next stage of the journey, nor how long before he will get there ; hasn't an idea what this place or that is particularly or incidentally noted for, and can lie down to his evening's repose with perfect contentment if he never *should* know. By this means he is left free to absorb the guide-book and the conversation of those about who do know, and thus is thoroughly posted on all matters of the route both in the aggregate and detail, and

"Fourth. He is without courtesy to his own sex or gallantry to the weaker. Thus being voted a boor by general consent, he may always secure the most desirable seats and corners in conveyances, the best seats at the tables—where he can reach the choicest dishes—and the first choice of rooms at the hotels. No one will borrow his newspaper or his magazines, or interrupt him in their perusal ; no one will sample his favorite cigars or imbibe from his—medicine flask. In short, he must be stupid, selfish, conceited, and 'cheeky' beyond compare. When you have learned and can practice these simple rules with ease, my dear fellow, you may consider yourself an accomplished traveler, and people will look up to you and envy and admire you—as they do me."

And the insufferable wretch stretched himself at full length on the only bench in the vicinity, closed his eyes in serene contentment with himself and the balance of the world, and was asleep in a moment. I shall wake him directly to learn all about Washington and Mount Vernon and the other big fishes of the Potomac, with whom he is better acquainted than old Baedeker himself. In the mean time this gallant ship continues to breast the bounding billow, and the man at the wheel is holding her strong to the windward, with her mainsail hard a-port and her bowsprit plowing the raging main. I am not sure about the exact nautical correctness of that last sentence; but being new to the marine service, I trust that any trifling inaccuracies of phraseology may be condoned, if not pardoned. I shall write you again from the first port we touch, and am, thus far,

Enthusiastically,

SAUL WRIGHT.

II

ON THE BEAUTIFUL BLUE POTOMAC.

STILL AT SEA, OFF POINT LOOKOUT,

POTOMAC RIVER, August 2, 18—.

THE final closing in of the night finds our expedition in the vicinity of Acquia Creek and about ᐧ
rounding Maryland Point, near which the Nanjemoy makes into the Maryland swamps. The
Lady is putting in her fifteen knots with painful regularity, and a good, round, able-bodied August
moon slowly climbing up out of the sacred soil of the mother-in-law of Presidents. The pilgrims are
gracefully disposed about the decks in picturesque groups, in which ham sandwiches and cold chicken
play no inconsiderable part, and the pop of the beer-bottle mingles with the song of the Potomac
turtle, and the voice of the tourist urchin whose name is legion as he vociferously howls for " more."
It is the hour that poets love, of which artists dream, and lovers in all ages and climes are wont
to claim their own ; the hour when Nature has retired to rest, and throwing " her sable mantle round
has pinned it with a star ;" the hour when the man

at the wheel peers out into the night, and watches for land and water marks that none but he can recognize; the hour when tender youth and blooming maids steal away to quiet corners of the boat, and sigh and spoon and breathe their secrets to the laughing moon. And, most important of all it happens to be the hour when our particular party has lighted its evening cigar after having put itself outside a respectable supper, and retired to the communion of its own thoughts. The Pharisee is contented with himself, and hence in good humor, and disposed to accommodate himself to his surroundings. I think he is satisfied with the conduct of the moon and stars, and willing to concede that he could not improve upon the situation.

"I never pass the mouth of the Nanjemoy," says he, "without thinking of a dark, pitiless night some fourteen years ago, when a frail bark—bearing the fortunes of two unfortunate wretches hurrying for shelter against a nation's vengeance, drifted by the current around Matthias Point, just rising below there on our starboard bow—was spied by a gunboat and chased to the woods of Nanjemoy.

"Just off our quarter, where the moonbeams are dancing on the tips of the waves, is the entrance to a narrow inlet that crawls for a dozen miles through the swamps, and ends at Port Tobacco. Just now

it is not much of a port, and doesn't see a hogs-
head of tobacco in a month. But in the days of
the rebellion it was a happy haunt for spies and
blockade-runners, the refuge for the criminals from
both armies, the home of the river thieves and pi-
rates, and generally the devil's own Elysium. The
natives were all rebel sympathizers, whose sympathy was cheap and harmless and inconsequential,
and it was not deemed by the government worth
the trouble and bother of occupation. Here Atzer-
ott flourished as a coach-maker, and Dr. Mudd carried on a little harmless practice against the chills
and fever, which, being an inheritance from their
fathers, the natives declined to tamper with. A
few miles up the country—a squalid settlement, to
which some mysterious some one has bequeathed
his initial—at T. B. was a huge, tumble-down tav-
ern, where Mrs. Surratt dispensed cheap whisky, and
caught an occasional traveler like Wilkes Booth
with plenty of money and a hobby, who scattered
the one while working up the deviltry required to
develop the other."

"Wilkes Booth—what a bold, handsome, devil-
may-care fellow he was, to be sure," interrupted
Jack. "I can seem to see his dark, melodramatic
face, that always suggested an idea of Lucifer—a
face that was Satanic in its beauty and pale with

the faint shadow of the coming tragedy. How often have I passed on the Avenue the woman who wrote of him that she would marry him at the foot of the gallows, and never without recalling the man whose fatal beauty and accomplishments could incite such devoted love and homage, to dim some little the horror of his crime. What a brilliant scapegrace he was! What a reckless, generous, whole-souled reprobate, whom the women spoiled by adulation and the men by envy. What a—but never mind. Go on, my dear Pharisee ; you were down at T. B., I believe, when I left you."

"Yes, thank you, if you are through—not that I would presume to interrupt your rhapsody, you know, only if I am to tell this story I prefer to do it in my own vulgar way. Well, it was into Port Tobacco that Booth and Harold rode on that fatal night when all the bitterness and malice and atroc- ity of a four years' struggle had culminated in his dastardly act, and its terrible story was flashing over the land, carrying terror and dread to the hearts of a nation. Here they spent the next day —Saturday—and Sunday morning, when, becom- ing timid on the news from Washington, they stole down to the ferry, some six miles below the town, where they were concealed until Thursday night. Then they attempted to cross over into

Virginia, lost their way, and were chased into Nanjemoy, where they were found by a poor farmer,
and shared his hog and hominy for a couple of
days. Saturday they were more successful, crossed
the river, and spent the night in the barn of Dr.
Stuart, a rich Virginian of Westmoreland County.
From here they crossed the Rappahannock, steal-
ing gradually toward the rebel lines, and picked up
Willie Jett, a Confederate captain, who piloted
them to Garrett's farm, within three miles of Port
Royal, and then seeking his own safety, was
pounced upon by Doherty with his squad of the
16th New York Cavalry. Jett squealed before he
was hurt, showed them the way to Garrett's, and
on Wednesday, the 26th of April, after eleven
wretched days of pain and anguish, Booth met his
Nemesis in Boston Corbett."

Now we have passed the light at Cedar Point,
and a little later are off the mouth of the Wicomico,
opposite the entrance to Pope's Creek, between
which and Mattox Creek is the birthplace of Washington. I hesitate long before opening the flood-
gates of Sid's eloquence, which I knew would be
carried away with a rush at the slightest allusion to
the locality; but Sid himself, as if awaiting the precise moment when the blessed opportunity would
present itself, has primed himself for the occasion.

"Seventeen hundred and thirty-two," says he—and I knew it was coming—"one hundred and forty-seven years ago.

"The Potomac," he goes on, after affording us the opportunity to gulp down the emotion which his dismal reference to the historical date was intended to excite, "The Potomac is particularly associated with the private life of Washington, her banks having listened to his infant prattle—if it be possible to associate an infant's prattle with the immortal first in war, etc., etc.—and to his dying whispers. What the Potomac does not know about Washington isn't worth mentioning. Her sands furnished the material with which he first constructed the mud pastry of childhood—always presuming that he ever was a child, and I confess the presumption is unpardonable—her waters enjoyed the enviable position of purveyor to his table, and to her broad bosom he stole away on Sunday afternoons when the paternal laid the flattering unction to his soul that George and his brothers were imbibing wisdom in the Sunday-school. Here we are pained to note a glaring dereliction of duty on the part of the aforesaid Potomac, in not having gathered him in as a penalty for disobedient and surreptitious desecration of the day. It is not in accordance with the Sunday-school books that the

Muse of History should have interfered, and have provided a career for a youth who went sailing on Sunday afternoons. It was wrong—painfully, pitiably wrong.

"It was along the banks of this beautiful Potomac that the youthful G. W. wandered at twilight, hand in hand with some village maiden, into whose blue eyes he gazed in rapture as he poured into her ears the tale of his first and virgin passion, and pressed her waiting lips in the tender, timorous ardor of first love. Here they sat down by the river side and watched the silvery moon as it danced on the rippling waves, and built brownstone fronts in the atmosphere, and projected bridal tours to Saratoga and Coney Island, and figured out the expense of a Cook's Tour to the Holy Land. And then, when the night was far spent, and the moon had turned in, and the barn-yard birds were crowing the small hours, they wandered homeward and swung their good-nights across her front gate. Alas! parting was such sweet sorrow that they could say "Good-night" until 'twere morrow. But it is too painful to pursue these harrowing reminiscences. We all know their melancholy end, and that the course of true love never ran smooth. He was soon called upon to play a star engagement on the stage of life, and furnish an example to coming ages, and she—well, she wasn't, and that's all history has to say on the subject. Doubtless she never told her love, but let concealment, like a potato worm, prey on her damask cheek. It required a considerable cheek in those days for a Virginian maiden to angle for a husband. There were no watering-places in the seventeen hundred and forties, and the White Sulphur Springs and Old Point had not even been thought of."

"Sid," said the Scribe, interrupting the flow of that worthy's eloquence, to his intense disgust, "did I ever tell you of my visit to the birthplace of Washington? No? Well, I'm not proud of having enrolled myself among the famous explorers whom history will love to honor; but among the many delinquencies of my long and eventful career I am ashamed to confess that I once visited Westmoreland County, in which rocked the cradle of the infant George."

"Did you, indeed? But I have no doubt of it. You are young and foolish, and, I presume, patriotic. I have always desired to know about Washington's birthplace, and have lived in the confidence that sooner or later I should encounter some idiot who had taken the trouble to go there. How did you get there? Did you see the birthplace, and how much of it did you bring away?"

"I came, I saw, and I haven't the least hesitation in saying I was conquered. And if Cæsar and his legions had ever met a squadron of Potomac mosquitoes on the field of battle, he would never have crossed the Rubicon but once. I presume the late General Cæsar had a hard march into Gaul; but if he had ever marched over a Virginia road he would have surrendered to the first Goth or Vandal he met. The fast-sailing clipper-ship that bore me to the scene was called the *Hi. Livingstone.* I shall ever hold the name in grateful remembrance, and ever associate it in my memory with the infernally *low* living that distinguished its table. Washington and Hi Living! Hi Living and Washington! Remarkable combination! The one emblematical of the soaring eagle, the other of the creeping turtle. The one rose from the muddy banks of the Potomac and reached the summit of fame; the other started from the nation's capital and landed in the Potomac mud. You see it was merely a transposition of terms.

"Well, you know I had been told before leaving Washington that the nearest landing-place to the sacred spot where the illustrious first saw the light was Wirt's Wharf on Mattox Creek, a distance of some ten minutes' walk from Wakefield, so that, when reaching the vicinity of Mattox, it was no more than reasonable that I should have suggested to the captain of the *Livingstone* the feasibility of putting me ashore at the festive spot in question. *Livingstone*, I should explain, was the name of the craft that bore my fortunes to Westmoreland County. I have forgotten the name of the captain, but I presume it must have been Hi. Living also.

"'Where did you want to stop?' remarked the captain. 'Wirt's Wharf? Condemnation! do you suppose I am going to swing up against every wood-pile along the river?'

"Now, as the principal occupation of the *Livingstone* since leaving Washington had been to swing up against everything that looked like a wood-pile, I didn't exactly catch the drift of the captain's remarks, so I merely remarked in that humble tone in which a poor landsman always addresses a sea-captain, 'Yes, sir, if you please—at Wirt's Wharf. I desire to visit the birthplace of Washington.'

"'D—n Washington!' said the autocrat of the *Livingstone*. 'What inell do yer want to go there for? There's nothing to see any way but an old corn-patch. I am not going to stop at Wirt's Wharf. I'll put yer off at Currioman,' and in the innocence of my heart I permitted the *Livingstone* to carry me on to Currioman.

"Currioman is the name of a variety of geographical divisions located just opposite Blackistone
Island, about fifty miles from town. There is Currioman Bay, Currioman Creek, Currioman Point,
and last, but not least, Currioman. It was into
this geographical labyrinth that the *Livingstone*
floated somewhere about midday, and after an in-
terminable series of backing and filling, managed
to stick fast in the mud within a stone's throw of
the crazy structure that is dignified with the title
of Currioman Wharf. There were several ways
that suggested themselves to me to overcome the
situation. I might have jumped overboard and
swam back to town, I might have bored a tunnel
through the mud to shore, or thrown a suspension
bridge from the hurricane deck of the *Livingstone*
to the wharf, or been blown ashore from the mouth
of the cannon; but none of them seemed altogether practical. I offered the engineer a dollar to
blow up the boiler, trusting that in the general
disintegration of matter I might have turned up
somewhere near the birthplace of the first in war;
but he spurned the tempting bait with the strong-
est of nautical emphasis. The inhabitants of the
town of Currioman—two small boys and the post-
master—stood on the wharf and cheered us till
supper-time; then they went home, and the mos-

quitoes cheered us till morning. It was altogether a jolly time.

" Let me bridge over the chasm of that unhappy night and the following morning in a sentence. It was slow, tedious, and melancholy—almost as slow, nearly as tedious, and quite as melancholy as the animal I procured at Currioman to carry me to Wakefield. Nine miles of the most wretched road that human nature ever conceived to torture a traveler; three miles of the muddiest, boggiest mosquito-infested cow-path on earth, and the end thereof is the Mecca of America. A lonely quarter of an acre on the bank of a sluggish stream, a group of cedars and a mass of brambles, one solitary fig-tree and a big stone quite overgrown with weeds, and a perspective of cow-fields and potato patches. Only this and nothing more. But I stood on the spot where rocked the cradle of the Father of his Country. I hung my harp on that rheumatic fig-tree and I wept. It was a good place to weep. It was gloriously, grandly, and thoroughly retired, and I needed a relief to my feelings. I had journeyed in the pursuit of a sacred memory, and I had found it. On that rude bowlder at my feet was emblazoned the mortifying fact that here was born the first President of the Republic, and in that inscription was explained the family motto, '*Exitus acta probat.*' I was devoutly thankful to feel that the Latin tongue afforded fitting phrase to apologize for the humiliation of having been born in Westmoreland County."

"What an admirable motive," says Dick, as the Scribe concludes his tedious narrative. "What an admirable motive for an historical study. I really think I must do something for posterity by transferring the scene to glowing canvas. Couldn't I work in an allegory or something of that sort? The dreary surroundings are emblematic of the wretched and forlorn condition of the colonies, at the moment when the coming hero was brought into the world amid fear and trembling. The lonely spot beside the sluggish stream, where the willows weep, and the long river-grass sways in the listless winds, is indicative of—of—what in the mischief are they indicative of, any way?"

"Chills and fever," suggests Jack.

"Well, no," responds Dick in all seriousness. "I don't think I could well express that in an historical study. Then there are the corn-fields and the lowing kine—that's agriculture—the majestic Potomac in the distance, white with snowy sails— that's commerce. Then I might work in the Genius

of Liberty, and the rising sun—the dawning of a
new era, and—"

"And Saul hanging his harp on the fig-tree, and
weeping because there were no more mosquitoes to
conquer." This from Jack. "Commence it, Dick,
commence it by all means, and get it off your
mind."

"Saul, my boy," says the Pharisee, "you are a
hero and a martyr. Such perseverance as yours
discovers North Poles and penetrates dark conti-
nents. But you lack enthusiasm, my boy, you lack
enthusiasm," and Sid lapses into thought. I am
not sure, but it is my firm impression, justified by
sundry sounds of a purely nasal character, that
my story has had a tendency to send Sid to the
land of dreams.

About midnight we swing away from the course
of the river into a broad inlet, where a long line of
many-colored lights and a dim background of sug-
gestive woodland marks the situation of Piney
Point. We are not impressed with the beauty of
this hermaphroditic watering-place from a bird's-
eye view from the deck of the *Lady*. To be sure
the hour is midnight, and the denizens have doubtless been turned out from their beds to perform
the nocturnal duty of receiving possible accessions
to their number from town, and candle-light is not

particularly conducive to those tints and charms
that are expected to attend the path of beauty.
Nor is the process of endeavoring to look happy
and contented with the countenance, while fighting
mosquitoes with both hands and feet, a movement
attended with that grace and dignity which should
mark the carriage of pleasure-seekers at a would-
be fashionable resort. And as we back out from
the crazy old pier, and the twinkling lights fade in
the wake of our churning paddles, we charitably
conclude that we have caught Piney Point at a
disadvantage, and are not disposed to be over-
critical. Handsome is, perhaps, as handsome does.
And thus we steam away into the night, and take
up again the widening channel of the Potomac,
with Point Lookout light just glimmering in the
distance, and a clear August moon lining a radiant
pathway on the waters, as if tracing the careless
course of our pilgrimage.

Drowsily,

SAUL WRIGHT.

III.

By the Sad Sea Waves.

Old Point Comfort, Va.,
August 8, 18—.

WE are lounging on the parapets of the fortress, with the cool sea-breeze playing about us, and a fervent August sun pouring its beams on our devoted heads. Before us lie the rollicking blue waters of Hampton Roads, dancing and surging in the sunlight, one vast stretch of swelling waves ; where the waters of the James, the York, the Nansemond, the Rappahannock, and the Potomac have joined hands with the Elizabeth and the brave Chesapeake, and are hurrying away to the sea. Here, they are rolling in fantastic waves, with foamy caps, that bow and courtesy and pirouette in the sunlight, and chase each other in merry, romping glee to the shore, where they break and bubble on the silvery sands. There, in illimitable volume of blue and green, far to the eastward, they are sweeping away to the sea ; glimmering beyond the low head-lines of Sewall's Point and Bayview ; gliding between the twin capes Henry and Charles,

who stand like grim sentinels at the gateway of
the watery avenue that leads to the nation's capital, to the broad ocean that washes the shores of
the hemispheres.

Teeming with life and beauty is this glorious
roadstead. Studded with white sails, from the
stately merchantman that bears her snowy canvas
in the pride of strength, to the skimming yacht,
the puffing steamer, and the fisherman's yawl; the
smoke of commerce and of peaceful pleasure that
mingles with that from huge guns at target practice, and forms fantastic clouds above our heads.
To the left the spires of old Hampton are gleaming
in the distance, the low-lying sand-spit, with picturesque cottages dotting the long white bar that
stretches along the shore line to the threatening
bastions of the fortress, the head-lines of the pen-
insula as they pencil on the horizon the way to
the York and the Nansemond. In the *entourage* are
Newport News, Big Bethel, Craney Island, the
gloomy Rip-Raps, Sewall's Point, and the broad
avenue that leads to Norfolk, Portsmouth, and beyond the naval station at Gosport, to the borders of
the Dismal Swamp. It is a picture that is unex-
celled, a panorama of land and waterscape that is
unequaled. And around and about the clear salt
fragrance of the sea, the balmy breezes, and the

genial sunlight of an August morning. For here, where every wave and point of land is bristling with war memories, the white-winged angel of peace has made her home, and concord and tranquility attend her gates.

It is to the midst of this halcyon scene that our Bohemians have wandered to the parapets of the fortress, and are lounging away the hours while the busy waves are moaning and murmuring about them. "All round the coast the languid air did swoon, breathing like one who hath a weary dream." They are at peace with themselves and the world; they have found a land of dreams without the fatigue of seeking it; they are contented without the trouble of expressing it.

"By the sad sea waves," trolls the poet, "I listen while they moan. They lament o'er graves of hope and pleasure flown."

"May the d—ickens fly away with you for a sentimental old cad!" shouts the Pharisee. "You have interrupted the sole idea I have had this morning. Now seriously, Jack, were you ever on the sea-shore in your life that you didn't tune up on the sad sea waves?"

"Jack is overwhelmed with the grandeur of the situation," interposes the artist. "Did you ever see a more charming picture, Sid, than now sweeps before you? It is a symphony in black and white, a living, throbbing inspiration, an idealization that no canvas can catch, no—"

"That's it exactly, Dick," says the poet, grateful for a re-enforcement; "don't you know when Coleridge speaks of ' ships and waves and ceaseless motion,' and all that sort of thing?"

"Yes, I remember a charming composition of Turner's, in which the waves and the sky seem to meet without any line to divide their illimitable—"

"Oh, you be blowed!" and Sid throws the last lingering inch of his cigar into the "symphony in black and white" with a gesture that speaks ill for his usually serene temper. "Turner hadn't the least conception of harmony in color, and Coleridge never saw the ocean in his life. Now, if you fellows really care to know anything about this 'living, throbbing inspiration,' as Dick has heard somebody say, I will give you a few leaves from the romance of Hampton Roads. But no poetical interruptions, Jack, or I'll throw you out among the 'sad sea waves,' that you may listen while they moan," and Sid squares himself for a masterly effort.

"This broad, surging expanse of water that spreads out before us," says he, "this immense watery plain where fleets may maneuver and navies may ride at anchor, is Hampton Roads. Can any of you tell me why a body of water should be called a road?"

"Because it has a pebbly strand," says Jack.

"Because navies may ride at anchor, of course,'' shouts the artist, astonished at the ignorance of our poet.

"Is it anything about breakers?" inquires the latter. "Don't people break stones on the road occasionally?"

"You should know, if any one," interposes the Scribe. "Go on, Sid, we all give it up."

"It was into this grand estuary, one morning in May, two hundred and seventy-two years ago, that the lost ships of Newport, sent out as foragers from Gosnold's fleet in Massachusetts Bay, glided to a sure harbor of refuge. Just in front of us they turned their prows to the northward, seeking a firm landing-place, and wandering through the broad mouth of the York, they first set foot on American soil, where a cosy inlet made in from the river, and luxuriant foliage came down to the brink of the waters. And in compliment to their king they named the spot Jamestown. And here a few years later came brave Captain John Smith, who organized the infant colony, and ruled over the new dominion with an iron hand. Here too came sturdy

Powhatan and his lovely daughter, the fair but dusky Pocahontas, and—"

"Why, of course," interrupts the poet ; "didn't I see John Brougham do the drama of ' Pocahontas ' at Wallack's? Fanny Davenport was Pochy, and she danced a break-down, and her father killed Smith with a stuffed club, and then she married somebody, I believe it was Smith, and became the mother of all the Smiths in America."

"You are wrong, Jack," said the artist in a patronizing tone. " Pocahontas married a fellow by the name of Rolfe, and the whole story is deline-ated on glowing canvas and hangs in the rotunda of the Capitol at Washington. The *chiaro-oscuro* of the work is most striking, the pigments being ad-mirably disposed, and—"

"And the price was ten thousand dollars," says the Pharisee. "The best paint was worth a thou-sand dollars a pound when the Pocahontas cartoon was painted, and it required just ten pounds for the job. Chapman threw in the labor of putting it on to bind the bargain. Now if you youngsters will let me go on with the historical business, I shall be gratified. Where was I ? I believe I had disposed of Pocahontas, or rather Jack had married her to Smith, and— oh, yes. Well, in the year of 1620, the same year

4

that the *Mayflower* landed at Plymouth, a small
Dutch trading-ship stole silently in through this
very roadway, bearing a cargo to become the curse
of the country—that demon of all mischief, African
slavery. There is an historical coincidence in the
fact, that on this very spot where we are now
lounging, two hundred and forty-two years later,
within sight of the spot where the first cargo of
slaves was landed, Ben Butler formed the first camp
of contrabands, destined to become a camp of freed-
men. Who shall say there is not poetic justice in
the eccentricities of fate? Here again, on one
eventful morning when the sun shone as brightly
as now, and these same moaning billows were dancing in the sunlight, a huge, terrible monster darted
out from the mouth of the Elizabeth, breathing fire
and destruction to the hapless wooden fleet that
rode proudly at anchor, and, secure in its invinci-
bility, dashed into their midst, dealing death-blows
and devastation they were powerless to resist ; and
here within our sight, the heroic Morris, disdaining
to strike his colors, went down with the *Cumber-
land*, with a parting salute to the starry banner that
waved defiantly from his sinking mast-head. And
still again, on the prouder morning that followed,
the brave little *Monitor*, unknown, untried, and un-
heralded, like a marine David daring to cope with

an invincible Goliah, steamed boldly and galiantly to the rescue, drove the monster *Merrimac* cowering to her lair, won the praises and admiration of the nations, and revolutionized the science of naval warfare throughout the world and for all time."

"Bravo!" says Jack. "You make me proud, old fellow. 'Columbia's the gem of the ocean,' ain't she? And so all that happened right in front of us. Pocahontas and Ben Butler and the battle of the iron-clads and all the rest of it. What a glorious thought, that standing on the battle-scarred heights of Fortress Monroe—aren't they battle-scarred?—with this glorious pond of water before me—this magnificent amphitheater wherein all the best dramas in our history have been enacted, I can plant my foot on this sacred soil, and raising my right hand toward Heaven, exclaim with—with —with some one, 'I, too, am an American!' By Jove! there goes my divinity in pink. By-by, boys. I'll see you at dinner," and as Jack descends the embankment and hurries along the sands, we can hear a clear tenor voice expounding a lament to the "sad sea waves."

Jack always has a "divinity in pink." I never knew of but one occasion when Jack did not have a divinity in pink, and on that emergency the divinity who, for the time being, had ensnared his susceptible affections, was robed in cerulean blue. I imagine, in the absence of a supreme passion, Jack would be inconceivably wretched. Jack is always wretched, for that matter; for, by some strange anomaly of fate, the divine creatures who for the moment have possession of his beating heart, either refuse to respond, as in duty bound, or have already responded to the heart-beatings of some other fellow. Still, Jack is never discouraged, inasmuch as the breezes that waft one beloved object from his gaze are quite as likely to waft another in sight. It is one of the compensations of Jack's existence that beauty is unlimited and illimitable. And so, as we watch him saunter down the beach in the wake of a merry party from the hotel, we feel confidence in the thought that the pink goddess is reasonably safe from the delirium of Jack's admiration.

"What a confounded idiot," says Sid, as the poet joins the party and takes up the line of march in the train of his pink divinity—" what a confounded maniac is a man in love—with a woman. I can understand why a man may become lost in admiration of an exquisite painting or a harmonious chord of music, like our friend Dick here, for instance. I can forgive him for losing his senses in the presence of a bit of nature, like these glorious Roads that dance and glimmer in the sunlight, and are bathed in the radiance of a thousand associations. I can sympathize with the Scribe whose loves are the loves of the poets, and whose mistresses come down to him from the middle ages, between the covers of some absorbing romance. But for a man in his sober senses to waste the precious moments of this fleeting life in making verses to his mistress's eyebrows, or in telling her that she is fair, or quoting sonnets to her frizzled hair, is unpardonable. For a reasoning, thinking male being to dangle in the train of a creature who is lovely because her powders and cosmetics and switches and ringlets have been artistically applied, and who is stylish and bewitching, because her *modiste* is a woman of taste, is a deliberate attempt to defeat the plans of the Creator, who made him for something better. I presume it is necessary that the male and the female should be on reasonably good terms with each other, and doubtless the ultimate fate of the species contemplates the episode of matrimony. I have frequently wondered why an all-wise Providence could not have formulated some plan whereby the world could be revolved without imposing upon the man the necessity of making himself agreeable to the woman. Mind you, I don't contend that the female portion of humanity may not be well enough in their way—and an absurd and mysterious way it is—nor that contingencies may not arise wherein expediency may dictate the desirability of improving one's condition by loaning one's name, and occasionally one's attachment, to some member of the sex aforesaid. It occasionally happens, you know, that a fellow is dreadfully in need of filthy lucre, or family influence, or something of that sort, in which event a desperate flirtation, an apparent affection, or even matrimony, may be a *dernier ressort.* I can conceive of such a situation, perhaps. But for a man in his sober intervals calmly, deliberately, and with malice aforethought, to surrender his self-respect, to plead, entreat, supplicate, lay siege to, and invest the female heart—whatever that may be —is a rank offense against high Heaven, for which there is absolutely no palliation. And as for a companion, you know, deliver me! Did you ever hear a woman say anything that was worth listening to? Did you ever know of one who would listen to anything but the smallest kind of small-talk, and be interested in anything but flattery of herself and scandal of her female friends? Bah! I have no patience with a man in love."

"Now see here, Sid," says Dick, "you have

either been jilted by some one of the charming
creatures at some time in your life, or—"

"Not a bit of it, my dear fellow. Do you imagine I would spend an hour of this limited existence
of ours in discussing love and matrimony with a
creature who has no conception of the meaning of
the one or the duties of the other, when I might be
—when I might be asleep for instance, or smoking,
or eating, or reading, or dreaming? Now I haven't
seen Jack's divinity in pink, and I probably never
shall, but I'll wager she hasn't an idea beyond the
determination of what particular toilet will be the
most taking for a particular occasion. Ten to one
she delights in pink for the reason that she would
be hideous in any other color, and a perfect fright
in white, and because Jack and the other moths
have a preference for fluttering around a pink candle. Now let's go in to dinner."

And we forget Jack and the pink unknown in the
discussion of one of Phœbus's incomparable feeds.
We are not epicures, although we have ideas regarding epicureanism that are based upon experience and possibly worthy of mention. Being unworthy *attachés* of that palladium of American
liberties—the Press—we of course dress in purple
and fine linen, and fare sumptuously every day.
But a dinner at Old Point Comfort is among the

most agreeable diversions of life. Nor could it
well be otherwise where the jovial Phœbus man-
ages the cuisine, and Dame Nature herself is his
cook. Fish, crabs, clams, and oysters in their over-
abundance swim to our kitchen windows and
absolutely beg to be baked, broiled, fried, or bat-
tered, that they may contribute to our comfort.
Teeming acres of melons, berries, and peaches sur-
round us, and square miles of market gardens and
orchards circumvent our abode. There must be
something in the sight of Phœbus that is provoca-
tive of hunger; of hunger that is ravenous, of appetite that is only appeased by scandalous indulgence. Or is it the strong sea-air and the salt
fragrance of the morning, and the sight of the blue
breaking waters of Hampton Roads? I am not
going to struggle over the problem, but the fact is
incontestable, that for good, square, solid refresh-
ment of the inner man, for bountiful banquets over
which the gods would have become enthusiastic,
there is nothing comparable to the tables of Hampton Roads, and the appetite imparted by their
saline surroundings. I am not drumming for the
Hygeia, by the way, nor heaping laurels on the
head of Phœbus, its jolly, round-faced, round-bel-
lied proprietor. Phœbus is a good-humored old
humbug. Phœbus is a marine monster, a nautical

Boniface, who pays no rent for one of the largest and finest hotels in the South, no taxes, no revenue, no license, no nothing; but whom every one pays to the limit of his income, and gives his promissory note for his estate after death. He laugheth the tax-collector to scorn, and the sound of the Moffett bell-punch ringeth not in his domains. He smileth upon his clerks and his steward, his man-servant, and his maid-servant, and the stranger that is within his gates. He counteth his gains from the rising of the sun to the going down of the same, and he pocketeth his little fifty thousand per season with the coolness of an iceberg. But he knoweth how to keep a hotel, and he hesitateth not to charge for the knowledge aforesaid, and I can swear to it if he leaves me enough to remunerate the notary.

"By the way," said Sid, as he poised a delicately browned tautog on the point of his fork and reached for the Worcestershire, "I had a trifling adventure this morning that Saul may as well record in the minutes. It was really of no consequence, you know, but it will help to fill the book, and Dick may draw from his imagination for a sketch. You see it was very early—long before sunrise—and I had taken a dip in the surf while waiting for Phœbus to open his bar-room, and concoct for me an eye-opener from a recipe which he asserts was left

him by a dying mother-in-law. I was a good piece
away from shore, you know, swimming against
wind and tide, and having an uncommonly hard
time of it, when I heard a timid little cry just ahead
of me that sounded peculiarly feminine and particularly distressing. Raising a trifle from the waves
and treading water with difficulty, I discovered a
strange little figure in a preposterous bathing-suit
but a few yards ahead of me, struggling with the
waves that buffeted it about like a piece of drift-
wood, and apparently without much resistance.
Well, of course I struck out for it, reached it without much trouble—caught it in my left arm—found
it was a woman and a ridiculously light weight—
put one of the little arms around my neck, and
made for shore. Had no time to see her face,
which was far down in the depths of a horrid sun-
bonnet—what scandalously ugly bathing-suits they
wear here, by the way—heard her say something
about 'sea-nettles,' 'cramps,' 'over-exertion,' or
something of that sort, and then I struck bottom
and we waded ashore. Then, making a graceful
little courtesy, she merely said 'Thanks,' and darting up the beach disappeared in the hotel. I went
out among the breakers again and—and why, by
Jove! that's all. To be sure, I had saved the life
of some poor creature that I would never recognize

if I met her in my own soup-dish; but it sounds
uncommonly tame, when I come to tell of it; I am
not certain but that I should apologize for boring
you with the mention of it. But upon my word, it
did really take the appearance of an adventure to
my mind, during its progress. Perhaps after all,
my boy, you had better say nothing about it in the
minutes. I apologize for the story as I would have
apologized to the apparition, had it given me a
chance."

As we were nibbling over the lingering remains
of the dessert, the beach party, with a good deal of
unnecessary bustle and hilarity, strolled into the
dining-room with a preposterously healthy and
hungry air that promised trouble for the larder of
the Hygeia, our tinted divinity bringing up the
rear with Jack beautifully in tow.

"How charming Miss Fisher is looking this
evening," said a gentleman at a table near us to a
lady companion.

"Miss Whosher?" said the party addressed, lev-
eling a single-barreled eye-glass at our unknown
goddess, who was looking up into Jack's eyes with
a most ravishing and wholly innocent glance of
inquiry. I imagine the soup had reminded Jack of
a line from Anacreon or some other equally classic
authority. "Do you mean that timid little thing

in pink? I don't agree with your adjective. A
decidedly vulgar taste—a most wretched combination! A blonde in pink! Where did you say she
came from?"

"Miss Fisher from Culpepper—General Fisher
—Army of Northern Virginia—impoverished—first
family," and the balance of this disjointed conversation was mingled with morsels of fish, crabs, and
oysters as they drifted down the throat of the gentleman at the next table.

"From Culpepper!" said Sid, as he sipped his
coffee, and frowned upon Jack and his fair enslaver;
"and from the First Families! It only needed
that to complete the farce. Jack is doubtless imbibing the doctrine of state's rights through a pink
straw. He is learning that the South was neither
whipped nor subdued, but merely overpowered by
a horde of foreign mercenaries. He is being informed that the Yankee is well enough in his
place, provided he doesn't infringe upon the divine
rights of his betters, but the true lord of the soil
and the born ruler of the nation is your fine old
Southern gentleman. He is monarch of all he
surveys, his pedigree none can disfigure; from the
Gulf to Delaware Bay he is lord of the soil and the
nigger. She's from Culpepper, and she dresses in
pink. Bah! Deliver me from the toils of an en-

chantress in dimity. As for Jack, I'm ashamed of him—and for that matter I'm ashamed of myself for having devoted so much of this blessed morning in discussing a woman in pink. Let us disinfect our brains with the fumes of an Intimidad."

And upon my word, my dear reader, I am also ashamed of having devoted so much of to-day's report to the episode of a woman in pink. But what would you have? As a veracious Scribe I am compelled to record the doings of the expedition. No one regrets more than I do the turn that its affairs are evidently taking. Jack, so far as the designs of the expedition are concerned, has deserted to the enemy. Dick at the present moment is sketching her profile from memory, and here is Thucydides, our philosopher, our mentor, our guide, turning the guns of his cynicism on the same petty object. I must assume the reins by a *coup d'état*, and move the expedition out of this dangerous locality. I shall certainly do it without loss of time.

Decidedly,

SAUL WRIGHT.

IV.

A Symphony in Red and White.

Old Point Comfort, Va.,
August 15, 18—.

I AM ashamed to say that we still linger at Old Point. I didn't assume the reins of management as easily as I imagined. Of course, I knew from the beginning it was a "gone case" with Jack, and counted upon his resistance. It is always a "gone case" with Jack, however, and I proposed to treat it with a decision and promptitude that would not involve any serious wrench of his heart-strings. Dick I considered a doubtful, who needed to be tempted with tales of a picturesque nature along the banks of the James or the Nansemond, or deluded with wild possibilities of the Dismal Swamps. But Dick has begun a study of Hampton Roads on a mammoth scale, which he asserts is to be the finest effort of his life, though why he requires so much practice upon female profiles I am at a loss to understand. I cannot see how any female figures can be worked in upon that vast perspective of Hampton Roads, but then I presume that being an artist—albeit an amateur—he knows what preliminaries are demanded to bring about the finest effort of one's life.

Upon Sid, however, I counted with certainty. I have never known so thorough a Bohemian as my friend Thucydides. I have always imagined him infested with the demon of unrest, and prepared at a moment's notice to pack his trunk for Chinese Tartary or the North Pole, to journey up and down the globe like a modern Wandering Jew, to ride, walk, sail, fly, swim, or whirl anywhere, everywhere out of the world.

Judge then of my astonishment when Sid met my advances with a strange hesitation, and when I pressed the point, came at me with those everlasting "lotos-eaters" who were once my particular favorites, but are becoming my positive *bête noir*.

"Why should we haste?" said he, in what I am positive was the bitterest irony under the circumstances. "Time driveth onward fast, and in a little while our lips are dumb. Let us alone. What is it that will last? All things are taken from us, and become portions and parcels of the dreadful past. Let us alone. What pleasure can we have to war with evil? Is there any peace in ever climbing up the climbing wave? Can you improve upon the climbing waves of Hampton Roads? Can you find any table to compare with that of Phœbus, or a landlord who can extract your last dime with a more smiling face? Jack is well enough. To be sure, he's madly in love with a pink costume, but then he'd be madly in love with a costume of some color or shade or tint anywhere upon this green earth. Then Dick has commenced a promising picture, and Dick only needs encouragement to distinguish himself. And besides, do you know I am a little anxious to discover who it was that I pulled out of the water that morning. Not that I care a picayune, you know, but then one doesn't like to be floored with a puzzle. I have scanned every female in this ranche, but hang me if I've found the right one yet. No, upon the whole, I think we had better remain for the present," and that settled it. Three against one is too powerful a majority to be overcome in the absence of a Louisiana Returning Board. So, as I have said, we still linger at Old Point.

Upon the whole I don't know that I regret it. Old Point is certainly a delightful resort, her dinners are enchanting, and the weather could not be improved upon. We have made flying trips to Hampton and Newport News; have run down to

the capes, and up to the field of Big Bethel;
we have fished all over the bay, and enticed all
manner of swimming and creeping things to our
net; carried the fortress by storm, and listened to
" Pinafore" from the Artillery School Band until
we can play it alone without a bower or a trump.
I have forgotten to mention that our party has
been increased by one, Jack's pink divinity having
taken an unaccountable fancy to that interesting
youth; though to her credit be it said, she has insisted that upon no consideration shall Jack separate himself from his friends. So to compromise
the situation she has taken our whole party under
her patronage, and leads us hither and thither, or
rather follows us here and there, or we all go together, or—in fact it seems to be a mutual thing all
around, and a mere matter of course that no one
thinks of bothering his wits about.

She is a bright little body, by the way; I wonder
if I could describe her. With no special talent in
that direction, I am afraid I shall make a mess of
it. In fact, I am sure of it; for how in the world
can one ever catch the lineaments of a face that
never bears the same expression for two consecutive moments, or attempt to delineate the meaning
of a pair of eyes that are wholly enigmatical? It
seems strangely ambiguous for me to say that this

5

vivacious little creature—who, for all that I know, may develop into a heroine — has an abundant wealth of auburn hair that is golden in tinge, and perpetually disheveled, a pair of black eyes that are always exhibiting some unexpected phase, a queer little nose that is decidedly *retroussé*, a mouth whose lips one has ever an irresistible inclination to kiss, and an infallible intuition that he never will, and who always appears in bewildering costumes whereof the motive is pink ; but that is really all there is to be said. Dick calls her "a symphony in red and white," and that seems to describe her with truth and condensation. To be sure, I might add that she is capricious, whimsical, and consequently more or less of a tyrant ; that she is a creature of moods, not all of which are based upon the strictest decorum ; that she is reckless, daring, and without a timid or cowardly bone, muscle, or nerve in her whole hundred-weight of femininity ; but these are personal traits of no particular consequence to a portrait. She is attended here by a middle-aged maid, whom Dick styles "a nocturne in umber," and who watches her mistress with the eye of a hawk, and by a white-headed, white-moustachioed old gentleman with a fondness for mint-juleps and draw-poker, and whom Miss Dora leads obediently about by the nose. Dick calls him "a

monochrome," "because he is so painfully and perfectly gray, you know."

Did I tell you her name was Dora? "The most
charming name in the world," says Jack, "for it so
thoroughly expresses my case. You know I *adore
her* to distraction," and I don't think there is any
doubt about that. Only if Jack had not adored so
many to distraction I should have more faith in the
permanency of his disease. As it is, I am not so
certain whether the adoration is mutual. Her
manner toward Jack is anything but affectionate;
but then, as I have said, she is a creature of moods,
and I never attempt to penetrate the mysterious.
She patronizes Dick, discusses music and painting
by the hour with him, upon which topics she leads
the conversation, which I regret to say our artist is
not always competent to follow, and by these es-
thetic chats, places "the finest effort of his life" still
further in the indefinite future. I am inclined to
think she is rather afraid of Sid, their discordant
natures appearing to clash without ever reaching
the limit of a dispute. They have never been
known to agree upon anything, though Sid's nature, being always courteous to a lady, renders any
breach of the peace altogether out of the question.
Although particularly garrulous to the balance of
our party, she seems to prefer to listen while Sid is

talking, and on several occasions has incurred
Jack's severe displeasure by forgetting to respond
to some thrilling and passionate burst from Schil-
ler in the midst of one of Sid's allegories. Upon
the whole, I am constrained to confess that Miss
Fisher, from Culpepper, is a decided acquisition to
our party.

We had been strolling through the streets of old
Hampton the other morning, where the elms and
buttonwoods form over-arching avenues, and quaint
old dwellings and churches buried in woodbine
peered out upon us as we tramped the venerable
streets, and lingered lazily along the dreamy lanes.
We had discovered a cosy nook beneath a wonderful elm, where a group of fig-trees hid us from the
chance passer-by—and the chances of passers-by
were infinitesimal—and a high hedge of acanthus
marked the boundary of some rustic retreat, whose
moss-grown lodge we had passed at the mouth of
the lane. There was a hamper set down in our
midst which the thoughtfulness of Phœbus had
dispatched to our relief, and from its capacious
depths the dainty fingers of Mademoiselle had ex-
tracted sandwiches and sponges, luscious bunches
of grapes, peaches that were exquisite, pears, plums,
and nectarines that were savory, and limes and
lemons that were merely incidental. A water-pail

had been borrowed from the mossy lodge, into which were cast cubes of translucent ice, handfuls of sugar, slices of lemon and crushed limes by the dozens. Into this strange compound the heads of several mysterious bottles were pointed, there was a popping of corks, a bubbling, a sparkling, a gurgling of fluids, and, rising triumphant over the seething decoction, Sid lifted a glass toward the zenith with a shout, and drank to "the health, the happiness, and the perpetuity of Old Point Comfort." Then we threw ourselves on the grass where the sunlight filtered through the abundant foliage, lighted our cigars, with Mam'selle's kind permission, and wondered if these hedges and fig-trees concealed the gardens of Hesperides.

"Gentlemen," said the old general as he puffed lazily at his weed, and bared his shining pate to the languid breezes, "this is really something like the days before the war. I believe I am growing young again under the influence of the moment. Ah, then there was nothing like the comforts of an old Virginia home. Would I could welcome you to the hospitalities of such an one as was once mine own. But the fortunes of a cruel war, the devastations of friends and enemies, have left me alone in my old age to fight the world alone and unaided."

"Indeed!" exclaims our symphony in red and white. "So I am nothing and nobody, I presume. I admit I am not a man of war to fight the world as you say, but to be left out of the fight altogether is altogether too much, and altogether cruel, and—"

"Who and what do you want to fight?" interposed Jack. "Who says you are going to be left out of anything? Show me the wretch that I may visit him with terrors dire and dreadful."

"Why, here is papa saying I am nobody and nothing, and—"

"But you are everything and everybody," responds Jack in a stage whisper, at which we all laugh, and Miss Dora frowns, and the little nose attempts the impracticable feat of turning up higher.

"Miss Dora has nothing to do but to continue to be charming," says Sid. "Jack will continue to be silly to the end of the chapter. You were speaking of the days before the war, general," he goes on, "and I admit with you that the times have changed—but have we not changed with them? *Tempora mutantur* you know, and so forth, and so forth, and so forth. I am forcibly reminded of changes in the history of Old Point. Twenty—thirty years ago it was the leading summer resort south of Saratoga, and divided with Newport the claims to supremacy. Here came the beauty and the chivalry from the Carolinas and the Gulf to meet the landed aristocracy from the Old Dominion. Here came the Masons and the Butlers, the Rhetts and the Hamptons, to meet the Fairfaxes, the Hunters, and the Lees. Here came Tyler and Clay, Calhoun and Gilmer, Barbour, Thompson, Upshear, and the Kennons, to discuss politics and poker, and solace the intricacies of diplomacy and mint-juleps. Here came the youth of the sunny South, to flirt, flaunt, and flutter, as for like purpose their brothers and sisters of the North sought their Saratoga and Nahant. And in their train came their ebony households, and Sambo lounged at his ease among the green fields, where a generation later came the ubiquitous Butler to organize the first camp of 'contra-bands,' and 'by an epigram,' as Winthrop says, to relieve this fair land of the curse of human slavery. Here was love-making and politics, cards and coffee, the juice of the grape and the essence of the corn, the bathing-suit and the evening toilet, the ball and the promenade, fair women and brave men, where eyes looked love to eyes that spake again, and all went merry as a marriage-bell until—boom ! went the guns of Sumter, and the curtain fell to quick music.

"Then came a period when the quiet sands of
Old Point awoke to the sound of tramping feet and
martial drums, and the hurry of massing troops,
and the embarkation of animals and munitions of
war, the booming of cannon and the creaking of
sails.   To the glitter of fashion had succeeded the
blue uniform and the clanking of sword and bayo-
net and the rattling of chains ; after the choice banquets and the bubbling of champagne came the
musty hard-tack, the stubborn salt junk, the muddy
coffee, and the rollicking canteen.   Where the flush
and glow of health and prosperity, in youth and
age, had landed at the old pier, and silks and rib-
bons had followed immaculate linen and shining
broadcloth down the plank walk to the hotel, now
came the dusty, grimy, and stern-visaged war veteran, the sick, the wounded, the dead, and the dying, the hospital matron and the cruel surgeon.
And then, in long, pitiful lines of emaciated, starv-
ing wretches, came the paroles from Andersonville
and Salisbury and Florence, and the old shores
surged and moaned, and wondered in their quiet
way when the end would come. And it came at
last—when men and treasures had been swept
away, when houses had been devastated and hearts
broken and families severed, and the demons of
hell were weeping over the only compensation

afforded for the unholy conflict—the loosening of the chains of the oppressed, to live for evermore in the sweet air of liberty."

"But that involves a difference of opinion, my dear sir," said the general, whose eyes had been flashing toward the close of Sid's peroration, "a decided difference of opinion. That involves a question—"

"It involves a question of dinner, my pugnacious papa," and our divinity springs to the rescue. "I confess that my hunger for the substantials of life exceeds my indignation, and my animosity is quenched with a draught of this excellent claret-cup. It is so brave, you know, papa, to attack a fallen enemy."

"I humbly crave the enemy's pardon," said Sid, with his stateliest bow, "and I second the motion for dinner."

And so we strolled back to Old Point; wandering down the dreamy old lanes, lingering a moment to peer into some shady church-yard, quizzing the natives, and pelting impertinent canines who dogged our passage with noisy bark; down through the dusty streets and along the sandy causeway, until the grand old roadstead burst full upon us, gleaming and glimmering in the sunlight, surging and moaning and refusing to be comforted.

"I am not altogether decided," said Sid to me that evening, as we stretched our legs on the balcony and watched the moon slowly sinking below the Maryland shore, "how to properly classify our new friend from Culpepper. I am disposed to think she is a fisher of men; her appropriation of Jack would indicate that, and she permits Dick to dangle in her train, as well as a dozen others of the gilded youth that honor this caravansary with their presence, and I am reasonably positive that she doesn't care a picayune for the whole dandified lot. There is nothing pretty about her; in fact, she hasn't a single regular feature; her mouth is awkward, her nose pert, her eyes indefinite, and her hair—great heavens !—her hair is preposterous. It is never arranged, for that matter, and its color is horrid. Well, I don't know about that. I rather like the shade of it, upon the whole, and perhaps its disarrangement suits her style better than though it were merely twisted into a ridiculous Grecian bob, or smoothed down over her forehead."

"Certainly—yes, to be sure," said I, not caring to discuss the subject of a woman's beauty with the most absolute woman-villifier in my acquaintance. "She looks well enough, for that matter, and she is certainly an excellent addition to our party. But, Sid, did you ever see a more charming picture than these Roads in the moonlight? I am prepared to admit that of all spots within my knowledge there are none comparable with this."

"Yes, I was saying as much to Miss Fisher last evening. She is enraptured with the place, of course, and has some little claim upon it as being within her own beloved kingdom. She has an excellent eye for the beautiful and the picturesque in nature, I am bound to admit that, and what a fiery spirit she has, by the way. Did you notice her eyes flash when I struck at her pet superstition this afternoon at Hampton?"

"That is perfectly natural, of course. She could not have done otherwise, and you must make due allowance, Sid, for people's prejudices, you know." Why will the wretch persist in discussing Miss Fisher? "Do you notice how the headlands of Sewall's Point stand up against the horizon? And what a magnificent avenue of brilliancy is formed by the moon's rays tipping the waves. It seems as though one might stroll a-down it on an evening promenade to the Capes."

"So it does, my boy, so it does. Did you ever notice that the moon's red rays as they fall on the water, assume a tint not unlike the hair of the Fisher? I have heard of moonlit hair, but I don't know that I have ever before encountered it outside of Ouida or Rhoda Broughton.   There is a peculiarity about human characteristics, do you know, that is strangely displayed in the texture and tint of the hair.   Now, is Miss Fisher's, for instance—"

"Oh, bother Miss Fisher!" I interrupt.   "Can you talk of nothing but Fisher, Fisher, Fisher?   I am hearing nothing but Miss Fisher from morning till night.   Jack is forever sighing like a furnace, Dick does nothing but study the various attitudes in which that estimable young female may be sketched, and now here are you, under the cover of your everlasting platitudes, prating of Miss Fisher's eyes, and Miss Fisher's hair, and—confound Miss Fisher!"

"With all my heart, old fellow, since she does nothing but confound me.   Between her and the mysterious nymph of my life-saving adventure I am thoroughly confounded, and puzzled, and perplexed, and driven to my wits' end.   Do you know I have been out in the surf every morning for the past week before sunrise and after sunrise.   I have even got up in the dim silent watches of the night and paddled about until morning, with no other result than several attacks of the cramps and incipient symptoms of rheumatism.   I am quite paralyzed with the attentions of the sea-nettles, and nearly pulverized with the buffeting of the surf. I really believe the sea-nettles imagine they have got hold of a bonanza, so constant have been my attentions to Father Ocean, and all to no purpose. It looks very much as though I should go down to my grave in blissful ignorance of the identity of the fair creature who did me the honor of permitting me to save her from the fishes of Hampton Roads."

" But is there no other way to identify her ? Did you not discover the color of her hair, the general idea of her figure, her size, her manner as she ran up the beach ?"

" My dear fellow, I haven't a single fact upon which to build a theory. She was, and then she was not. She came and she disappeared, and that's all there was of it. The dim twilight, the suddenness and the excitement of the moment, her preposterous costume, and her unexpected flight, all combined to render the whole affair to be merely a dream, a memory, an illusion. I am inclined to say, a delusion. There is but one way by which I could ever be sure that it was not a delightful nightmare, and that sole possibility is too absurd to be entertained for a moment. You see while I was bringing her ashore I held her by my left arm, while I drew her arms about my neck, and in that journey, a mere matter of two or three minutes, she clung to my neck with the grip of an octopod. Now then—"

"Yes, now then, you propose going up and down the land calling upon females of all ages and color and previous conditions of servitude to be kind enough to throw their arms about your neck, and droop their heads gracefully over your shoulder, in order that you may determine whether or not they ever enjoyed that enviable distinction before. A sort of a Cinderella business, you know. Sid, I'm ashamed of you."

"Yes, and I'm ashamed of myself; but, as I said before, I'm wholly puzzled and confounded, and— by the way, I had almost forgotten. Isn't that the band in the dining-room? I had promised a waltz to Miss Fisher. *Addios.*"

Now isn't this a nice position for the Scribe of a stag party? First Jack deserts us for a pink goddess, then Dick follows suit, and now here is Sid proposing to embrace every female in Virginia until he finds one that can hug like an octopod! What am I to do? How can one perform the duties of a Scribe with nothing to scribble about? I presume I might fall into line with Jack and Dick. If I could only act as a deputy to Sid now—but, of course, that's out of the question. But what then? I shall have to sleep on it, and in the mean time I am

Distractedly yours,

SAUL WRIGHT.

V.

THE MOTHS AND THE CANDLE.

NORFOLK, VA., August 20, 18—.

A BRAVE, busy little seaport in Southern Virginia. A broad, surging river—that glimmers and
glistens under a persistent August sun, and on
whose bosom huge ships ride at anchor. A long,
winding water front, where mammoth warehouses
and capacious sheds lead down to broad piers
where ocean steamships are embarking the spoils
of generous fields, and rusty sloops and luggers and
trim coast-wise craft of every degree lift a crowded
forest of masts and shut out the vista of cool
groves on the further bank. Noisy ferry-boats with
much bluster and hurry are plying limited voyages,
and spluttering tugs with spiteful puffs and wheezes
fill up the pauses. In mid-stream a few ocean
ships are contentedly waiting, and far a-down the
river a monster line-of-battle ship, beside which all
others seem as pigmies, stands out against the
horizon. Heaping drays rattle over noisy pavements, and noisier draymen urge unaspiring mules
to unsuspected speed. Busy tradesmen are decor-

ating shop-fronts with tempting wares, and howling hucksters crying incomparable goods at trivial prices.

Did I say busy? Ah, well! that was while we were near the water-front, and while the din of traffic and the bustle of commerce were ringing in our ears. We have strolled quietly down some narrow street, where high woodbine-covered walls shut in the privacy of homes, and rugged elms and buttonwoods over-arch the roadway. Here in venerable gardens, luxuriant fig-trees and oleanders struggle for existence among rose vines; there, sweeping willows, mossy with age and tired with the battle of life, live on, that climbing vines may mount and hide their decay with the plenitude of their youth; everywhere the delightful crape myrtle lightens up the picture with its pink crinkly blossoms. We are confronted with touches of mossy walls and quaint dwellings going proudly to decay, as though, having performed their purpose of being, they could await patiently the end of all things. Here the roadways are narrow and the sidewalks slender and thin, the yards capacious, and the porticoes airy; hammocks are swinging in seductive shades, and lawns clean-shaven invite to romps and relaxations of mind and muscle.

Did I say a Virginia seaport? Not a bit of it.

6

We have dropped suddenly upon some quaint old
town in the south of England, where the very air is
heavy with the mold of centuries, and these narrow sidewalks have been pressed by the feet of
Cavaliers and Roundheads. Why else should these
queer old rookeries, these fantastic ornaments to
dwellings and gate-posts, these grotesque doorways
and roofs, confront one at every turn? Why else
should these nondescript trades-people stand in
front their doors and exhibit their antiquarian
wares through ridiculous seven-by-nine windows?
Why else should the streets be named for titled
Englishmen dead and gone these hundreds of
years, and the door-plates assert in shining brass
the patronymics of families of whom no one has
heard since the days of Queen Anne? No—I am
positive we have happened upon a bit of the six-
teenth century, in these old streets of Norfolk, and
were it not for an occasional glimpse of a fashionable pull-back, and garments and hats that no female of that period would have been caught in
under pain of eternal punishment, I would be sure
of it. Now, too, the omnipresent darkey appears
upon the scene with the discordant cry of "Rags,
bones, and old iron!" an oleaginous Dinah shuffles
lazily by with a flock of pickaninnies in tow and
dispels the illusion.

I presume you are wondering why we are here. Well, so am I, for that matter, and am strangely uncertain how it all came about. The movement is enwrapped in a mystery that has so far defied my utmost endeavors to comprehend. Although delivered from the dangers of the briny deep, I am still all at sea, as it were, and prepared to accept almost any theory that may afford any solution to the mystery. You see, Jack came to me the other evening, just as we were about turning in, and suggested a moonlight stroll on the sands. Now, considering that Jack has seemed rather distant of late, and on one or two occasions has absolutely rebelled against the rules of the expedition, necessitating a reprimand which I felt myself called upon to administer, I presumed, of course, that the poet was about to unbosom himself of an apology and promise irreproachable conduct in the future. So, linking his arm in mine, I permitted him to lead me along the beach, as we discussed such leading topics of the day as seemed to come uppermost, in that constrained, hesitating tone which people always adopt when talking against time while awaiting a favorable opportunity to inject a leading question. Tired after awhile of this preliminary skirmishing, I thought it well to further an end of my own while giving Jack the desired opportunity to tender the *amende honorable*. So said I :

"Jack, old fellow, aren't you getting about tired of this place? Or are you intending to pre-empt a homestead, and settle down beneath your own vine and fig-tree on the sacred soil?"

"Well," said he, "I certainly could not select a more delightful spot, you know, nor can I conceive of anything more blissful in life than to spend it with the companion of one's heart and fortunes in a cottage by the sea, where the breezes are ever wafting the spices of the Indies, and the trees are ever sighing and the waves moaning and the birds —and the birds—the birds warbling, and—and— and all that sort of thing, you know. Where did you propose going from here, by the way?"

"Oh, well, for that matter I hadn't proposed any particular point. You know our plans were to have no plans at all. I had thought of suggest-ing a trip to the eastern shore with a day or so at Ocean City, and a tramp through the peach orch-ards of Lower Delaware."

"Well, I don't think much of that. Ocean City, they say, is the last place in the world, and, as for tramping through peach orchards I don't really feel equal to the effort. Ocean City is principally inhabited by mosquitoes, and peach orchards by bugs and all manner of creeping things that are eternally crawling down one's back, and building nests in one's hair and ears. Oh, no, you can count me out of that project."

"Well, what do you say to a trip to the Capes, where the breaking waves dash high, and the rocks come down to the sea, and the sounding aisles of the dim woods ring to the anthem of the free—eh?"

"Not any capes for me if you please, and I decidedly object to rocks coming down to the sea, or woods ringing with anything. If I am to listen to anthems I have a preference to hearing them in church by a paid choir of artists, and an organist of the first water."

"Suppose we compromise the matter then, and go down to Norfolk for a day or so, where we can mature our plans at leisure."

You see I was compelled to use a little strategy to get Jack away from Old Point. That was the first consideration, and it really mattered not at all where we went, provided the wretched fellow would consent to go at all. I was prepared to listen to all manner of remonstrances, and no little surprised that we were no nearer the apology than ever. Judge then of my astonishment when Jack shouted with what I considered unnecessary fervor—

"The very thing, old chap, the very thing! I was about to suggest it after you had exhausted your list. I didn't presume, you know, to seem to dictate; but I am afraid I have offended you by my perversity, and, upon the whole, we have had enough of Old Point, as you say. So suppose we decide upon Norfolk as soon as you choose."

Now I considered this right nice of Jack to voluntarily tear himself away from Old Point merely to oblige me, and I immediately forgave him all his little delinquencies, and took him back to my heart with effusion. Jack is not a bad fellow after all, if you only know how to take him, and I am satisfied that the pink divinity is merely an·episode.

Miss Fisher, by the way, had not made her appearance that evening. This was rather unusual, now I come to think of it, for that incomparable goddess had not heretofore permitted an evening to pass without holding her reception in the drawing-room, and forming a brilliant court in some corner, around which the majority of the male bipeds would cluster, while the female dittoes would arrange themselves into charming *parterres* of wall-flowers, and look daggers and frown columbiads and glare stilettoes. It had been a habit of our little goddess to bring about precisely

such a state of affairs as that, with every blessed
man and a few admiring members of her own sex,
congregated in some window-recess, or perched
demurely upon the stairs, like a flock of wild tur-
keys, when she would steal quietly away and join
our little party on the balcony, and then we would
stroll away into the moonlight or hide in some
corner of the pavilion, or mount the ramparts of
the fortress, where we would spread our wings and
soar up, off, and away to the fields of Bohemia.
Ah! those were hours worth remembering, and
upon my word I didn't blame Jack for regretting
them. In fact, I regretted the stern dictates of
fate which constrained me to insist upon a change,
and all the more did I appreciate the sacrifice of
our foolish young poet in leaving this delightful
scene to oblige what was merely, after all, an
absurd fancy of mine.

Very well. Returning to the hotel we encountered Dick, who I am sure must have been laying
for me, for I certainly can recall no occasion during our long acquaintance when that graceless
scamp was as effusive and gushing as now. "I
hope you are not tired, old fellow," said he, grasping my arm, and inserting a fragrant Regalia between my teeth as he extended the glowing end of
his own for a light. "I am anxious to consult you

regarding my picture, which you know I am positive is to be the finest effort of my life. Now you
see," said he, as we turned down the beach and
paced leisurely along the sands, "I have reached
that point in my work where I can leave the perspective and pin my whole attention down to the
details. It is to be more or less of a composition,
you understand, an oratorio in chromatics. I believe I have caught the inflection of the Roads, and
the tone of the sky, and the modulation of the
waves; in short, I have exhausted the glittering
generalities of this exquisite spot and—"

"I suppose you mean by all this, Dick, that you
are ready to move onward," I interrupted. Why
will some people always preface a communication
with an apology?

"That's it exactly. You see I know you fellows
are getting tired of Old Point any way, and are
only lingering to oblige me in the matter of the
picture."

"But where did you think of going, Dick?" I
inquire.

"Well, I have been told that there is no better
place to study marine effects in this vicinity than
—than along the Elizabeth—say at—at Norfolk,
for instance." This with a painful effort at indif-
ference. "Norfolk is quite a seaport you know,

and there's the navy-yard at Gosport, and all manner of craft are to be found along the wharves, and—not that I have any preference, you understand, only Norfolk is right handy, and as we haven't any decided plans, I thought perhaps you wouldn't object," and Dick puffed in silence as he strode along the beach with the air of a man who is perfectly indifferent to fate, but hopeful that fate will accord with his own desires.

"Well, Dick," I remark, after conning the subject in my mind, "I haven't the least objection to Norfolk, not the slightest in the world, only I am wondering a little at the wonderful unanimity between your thoroughly indifferent selection, and the equally unconcerned preference of Jack. By the way, did you notice the absence of Miss Fisher this evening from the drawing-room? I don't think she has put in an appearance since early this morning."

"Hasn't she, really? I hadn't noticed it. You know I have been busy with the picture, and— So it is settled we go to Norfolk. You are a brick, old fellow, and I am your devoted slave. Did you say that Jack wanted to go to Norfolk? I imagined him tied fast to the apron-strings of that charming little symphony in red and white. Ah! there's Sid ; I'll leave you to break it to him gently. Sid has such a ridiculous fancy for Old Point. Good night," and Dick vanished.

"Is that you, Saul?" said the Pharisee, advancing from the shadow of the pier. "You are just the one I am looking for. Have you a weed about you? Where have you been, and who has been with you? You needn't answer, for I don't care a cent, anyhow, except for the smoke, and I want you to join me in a promenade along the beach." Great heavens! thought I, what an astonishing mania for pedestrianism has suddenly developed among these lazy associates of mine. It is fortunate that we are about to get away from here, or I should be compelled to send back to town for another pair of boots. "Well, Sid, old chap, what's up?" I inquire, as with a sigh of reluctance I turn for the third time and take up the line of march for the antipodes by way of Newport News.

"I have been thinking over your desire to leave Old Point and move forward. I don't exactly like the idea, for I am contented, and I don't know where we shall ever strike another caterer equal to Phœbus; and the surroundings here are perfect, and the society altogether lovely. But I don't want to be selfish, my boy, and—"

"Had you decided upon the objective point, Sid?" This coincidence of magnanimity and im-

molation on the altar of friendship was overpowering, and I caught my breath for Sid's answer.

"Oh, no ; I haven't the least choice in the world.
Whenever I decide upon sacrificing myself for the
public good, I am absolutely indifferent to the
process. North, south, east, or west, whatever,
wherever, and whenever you choose. Only say the
word, and my satchel is packed for Europe, Asia,
or Ujiji. But, hold on now, come to think of it,
and as you seem to be asking my opinion, what do
you say to Norfolk?"

"Angels and ministers of graçe defend us ! Norfolk?" I ejaculated, catching my breath in fear and
trembling. "*Nemine dissentiente!* What demon of
coincidence has taken possession of you all? Perhaps you haven't any objection to backing up your
suggestion with a reason. Why Norfolk?"

"Well, I'll tell you why. You know I have never
discovered my naiad, the phantom of my morning
adventure. The mystery of that unaccountable
female is wearing on me imperceptibly but surely.
I am losing my appetite, growing small by degrees
and beautifully less, and it is a mere matter of time
when I shall degenerate to a living skeleton, and
all because of that haunting enigma that baffles
detection. Now you know drowning men catch at
straws, no less than drowning women, and the idea

has occurred to me that it is merely possible that my *incognita* may have come here from Norfolk the night before, gone out for an early dip in the surf, induced me to become her involuntary preserver, and returned home on the morning boat. There is nothing strange in the theory, and Phœbus tells me it is no uncommon thing for Norfolkians to run up here for a morning or evening bath. It is worth a trial, any way, and as you have asked my opinion, suppose we settle upon Norfolk. Now let's turn in, as it's past midnight. Break it diplomatically to Jack and Dick—ask their advice, of course, but if you love me, insist upon Norfolk." And so from the deck of the morning boat we looked our last upon Old Point.

Now here's the mystery of it. Why should these three separate and distinct individuals, with no collusion whatever, and under no restraint, either real or fancied, have suddenly and simultaneously determined to vacate quarters from which twenty-four hours earlier they could not have been driven, and locate themselves in one and the same town but ten miles distant ? Can there be some occult influence operating in our midst, having for its design the lives, the fortunes, and the sacred honor of these wretched associates of mine? It is altogether too much for me. With a solemn and premeditated determination to drift about the world, guided solely by our own sweet will, and setting fate at defiance, it looks very much as though fate had taken the matter into her own hands, and is proceeding to dispose of us without mercy.

   *   *   *   *   *   *

The plot thickens. I had closed this letter under the absorbing influences of the dinner-bell. I open it to advise you of further complications.

After searching the hotel from cellar to garret for a trace of my companions, and wasting a good half-hour in the process—during which period I existed under the agreeable state of mind that one enjoys in the knowledge that the soup is growing cold and the choice cuts of the joint becoming absorbed and non-existent—I entered the dining-room determined upon a game of *solitaire* with knife and fork that should strike terror to the hearts of both waiters and cook. I was received at the doorway by the affable African who commands the body-guard of hash-slingers at the Atlantic, and with a flourish as though I were the ex-President of the republic about to enter upon a Japanese banquet of fifty courses, conducted to a table laden with steaming viands and surrounded by the wretched fellows I had been searching, over whose feeding, and choking with laughter at some one of their egregious jokes, presided—the divinity in pink ! I was overpowered, struck dumb, annihilated with astonishment, and the details of that first dinner in Norfolk remain an aching void—a blank—the baseless fabric of a dream.

Not so, however, the delightful *tête-à-tête* that came in with the dessert, when all but myself had adjourned to the billiard-room for an after-dinner smoke, and the goddess in her graciousness had remained to bear me company.

"So you left Old Point," said she; "and of course with regrets."

"With regrets," I reply, "mingled with wonder why we left at all. You see I don't exactly comprehend, in the first place, why we are here; and, in the second, why you are here. I imagined you as the girl we'd left behind us, and ourselves as brutes for not paying our parting respects."

"But whose suggestion was it that induced you to come to Norfolk ?"

"Why, Jack I believe, in the first place, desired to change quarters, and, raising objections to everywhere else, induced me to suggest this as a last resort."

"But Mr. Longmeter was not the whole of you ; in fact, I always considered him to be in the painful minority. Did you invest him with the arbitration of your destinies?"

"Well, no; Dick was suddenly and unexpectedly attacked with a desire to study the marine picturesque, and deemed this pretty little port the only one on the face of the globe where it could be studied *par excellence.*"

"But that's only two of you. Did—did Mr.— I mean to say, why did—but of course the rest of you merely followed your friends as a matter of duty."

"Oh, no; Sid also, and so far as I know without any consultation with them, insisted upon coming here. To be sure he had an excuse which I regret I am not at liberty to repeat, it is so perfectly absurd; but what seems strange to me is, why this sudden fancy for Norfolk should have developed itself simultaneously, as it were, in the brains of those three graceless scamps. Just observe the coincidence. I am not at all superstitious, you know; but really this involves the weird, the mysterious, the—the—don't you think so?"

"Why, you foolish old fellow," says my goddess, with a most enchanting *moue*, "don't you understand that the mysterious loadstone that has attracted you all to this sublime retreat is none other than your most obedient and highly-flattered *vis-à-*

vis? I told Jack we were coming here, and I waved my handkerchief from the deck of the *Ariel* to the Pharisee, as he lay almost asleep in a little sail-boat just off Newport News. Parting, you know, was such sweet sorrow that I knew there was no need of saying good-by so long as you were all certain to be here on the next boat. Was I not right? Poor Scribe, the mystery was all in your own stupid head. They all knew we were coming here but yourself, and they adopted that means of bringing you here *nolens volens*. I am going to punish them by spending the afternoon all alone by myself at Brambleton."

But she didn't.

Confidentially,

SAUL WRIGHT.

VI.

DOLCE FAR NIENTE.

NORFOLK, VA.,
September 1, 18—.

WE are picnicking at Brambleton. A shady
knoll, whereover the reaching boughs of fragrant
cedars sigh in the scarcely-moving breeze, and the
salt fragrance of newly-cut meadow-grass comes to
us laden with the songs of meadow-larks and the
chattering of crickets. Nimbus and cumulus drift
slowly over a vast perspective of liquid blue, and
tiny flakes of vapor scud by, like advance couriers
of a coming storm. Movement there is little in the
sultry air; the tall field-grass nods languidly to its
neighbors across the way, and the marsh brambles
droop, and drowse, and wake with a passing breeze,
and tiny insect voices chant dirges to the dying
grass which the cruel scythe has laid in billowy
winnows all about us. And before us, always the
ocean, moaning and surging and breaking on the
sands, swelling and rippling, splashing, rolling,
tossing like one that hath a weary dream.

We are disposed in charming disorder in and

7

about the group of shambling cedars, secure in the
faith that the ugliness of our surroundings will re-
pel the advances of these ordinary mortals whom
each recurring trip of the little bob-tailed mule-car
is dumping upon the sands of Brambleton. We
are among them, and yet not of them. Our homes
are not their homes, nor our gods theirs. We are
a roving detachment from the army of Bohemia,
our weapons brush and pencil, and our countersign
"*Dolce far niente.*" Far in the land of dreams is the
gray old general, fighting again the enemies of his
bigotry, and living over the days that live only in
memory. In the limbs of a tall cedar, behold our
artist, perched in *alto-relievo*, striving to catch the
breadth of the sleepy meadows with their picturesque foreground of ebony reapers whose ragged
garments display all the colors of the palette.
Jack is reading aloud the stirring lines of "Morte
d'Arthur," to which the Scribe is the only listener,
and Sid is far away at sea, with a brush behind
either ear, and a water-color in neutrals that defies
him to catch the motive of those mirror-like waves
that glimmer and glisten, and are, and are not.
Mounting guard over the lunch-basket is Dick's
"nocturne in umber," drowsy with the effort to keep
one eye on her mistress while the other sleeps, and
shining with all the exuberance of an August noon-

tide. Our goddess, pink and bewitching as ever, has discovered a rustic arm-chair between the grotesque, gnarled roots of the cedars, and while seemingly deep in the pleasures of "Mirage," is watching Sid over its dainty black and red covers. She has thrown aside her jaunty *sombrero*, and as all the wealth of her abundant hair sweeps over her shoulders, a stray sunbeam steals through the cedars and touches it with a glowing hue that is among the lost arts and known only to Tintoretto. Dainty, winsome, captivating little goddess, may life be to you always as an August noon.

Mingled with the monotone of the locusts comes the clear voice of the poet, and the piping of a meadow-lark just under our feet.

> "And answer made the bold Sir Bedivere :
> 'I heard the water lapping on the crag,
> And the long ripple washing in the reeds.'"

"Never mind the reeds, Jack," shouts Dick from his perch ; "throw me up a piece of bread. I have got too much water in my foreground."

"Suppose you give me some of it," says the Pharisee, brought suddenly to himself. "It's water I'm in want of, with a whole ocean before me. What's the good of an ocean that won't keep still long enough for one to paint it ?" and Sid grasps a

brush in despair as Jack goes on with his narrative.

> "Ah, miserable and unkind, untrue,
> Unknightly, traitor-hearted. Woe is me!
> Authority forgets a dying king—"

"Why don't you throw me up the bread-crumb?"
shouts Dick again from the cedar.

"Authority forgets—authority forgets—where
was I? What does authority forget?"

"Forgot to throw me up something to mend my
foreground."

"Oh, confound your foreground! Come down
and get your own bread. How's a fellow going to
read a heroic poem, and other people listen, when
you are crying for bread up there in a tree?"

"Don't scold, Jack," says the goddess; "there
wasn't any one listening. What were you reading
about?"

"What was I reading about? Well, that's a nice
question. Where have you been, Miss Pink, may I
inquire?"

"Oh, me?" laughs the divinity. "Oh, I was just
climbing the Mount of Olives with *Constance Varley*.
What a stupid creature she was, by the way. The
whole of her story is told in a single line. *Il n'est
d'amour si triste, qui n'ait son maladie.* I am all out
of patience with some people."

"And so am I," cries the man in the main-top. "Am I to have any bread?"

"Bress yer heart, honey, yer shall have all de bread yer want, only we done got no bread. I'll frow yer up a sandwich in a minute," says auntie, who hasn't exactly mastered the situation.

"Did I understand your highness to say that the conduct of the Varley girl did not meet your approbation?" And Sid gave up the attempt to capture the ocean, just as a puff of air wafted his sheet toward the breakers. "If I remember correctly, Miss Varley engaged herself to one man while she loved another, imagining that the other would understand that she didn't care for the one, and would throw him over whenever she had captured the one she did love. A bird in the hand was decidedly better than another in the shrubbery. She merely argued from false premises. Wasn't that the Mirage?"

"I do not think," said her highness, "that you do my heroine exact justice. It was a mistake, you know, between her and *Lawrence*, and she suffered him to go, without a knowledge of the truth, rather than cross the barriers of what she conceived to be her modesty. Had she told him she did not love *Stuart*, there would have been an end of it. She hungered and thirsted for his love, and would not take the trouble to reach out her hand and take it. That is why I have no patience with her."

"But you really would not have had her confess her love to him when he had not asked for it? You would not have had her give what was not requested, would you? Miss Fletcher's story seems to me to be very prettily told, and she only stops the lips of her heroine when she could not say more with any regard for her pride, to say nothing of her modesty. In matters of love as in most else in this world, there are limits which the demands of society, the dictates of conventionalism, of womanly honor and pride, have set as a barrier. Thus far shalt thou go and no further."

"I don't care a fig for society, and were I in love I would have no pride, and certainly no hesitation in owning it upon the slightest encouragement. Whenever I love I shall be proud of it, and shall most likely be too unselfish to keep it to myself. Perhaps, as you say, no modest woman would throw herself at the head of the man she loved, but there are few things in this world to be had without asking."

"That's so, Dora, my love," says the general, arousing from his nap. "I have never known you to do without anything that asking for, and teasing, and begging for, would bring; that is, when you want it right bad. A more incorrigible tease never lived," he added, without any idea of the drift of the conversation.

"Papa is right," responds Dora defiantly. "Whenever I have set my heart upon anything, I always secure it. Whenever I really desire any-thing very much I shall not hesitate to ask for it. For instance, I am becoming very hungry, and am going to ask Aunt Jenny to rummage the lunch-baskets, and unless you are all very good, you shall not have anything, and you certainly will not with-out asking for it."

"What are you two quarreling about?" shouts Jack, who hasn't understood a word of the whole colloquy.

"We were discussing a theme of which you are totally ignorant, my boy," says the Pharisee. "We were speaking of modesty. Dick, old fellow, when you are through with that sandwich, throw it down, please. It is likely to constitute the sum and substance of our lunch."

Now our dusky servitor spreads a snowy cloth over the face of the earth, and distributes thereon fish, flesh, and fowl in homeopathic allowances, and fruits that are luscious and tempting without limit. Tennyson is put to sleep with "Mirage" on a bed of cedar spikes, and Dick's meadow study does obe-dient duty as a coverlid. The artist descends from his roost at the enticing jingle of the forks and spoons, and we recline at the banquet much after the custom of the ancient Romans, the result of which is painful cricks of the back, and somnolent eccentricities of the limbs, that induce us to tender the ancients aforesaid our heartfelt sympathies. We have learned from bitter experience that among the delights of this section of the universe, one needs to expect the blessing of water, pure and undefiled. I think there can be no doubt that the water in and around Norfolk has qualities that commend it to the mariner, and we have found it exceedingly convenient for bathing ; but we cannot believe that the Creator in his care and compassion ever designed that the villainous compound that goes under the name of water in Norfolk should ever enter the system. There is, however, a merciful provision for the emergency that is secured in glass vessels with a patent stopper, the prevailing tint of which is an exquisite brown, clear and transparent as amber, and as sparkling as the choicest Cliquot. We are not puffed up with pride, neither are we over-inflated with vanity. Hence we permit Gambrinus to preside over our feast with a dignity and decorum that is peculiarly his own, to say nothing of an economy that is peculiar to Bohemia.

"Now then," says the Pharisee, as he lifts a glass of foaming nectar, with a bow to the goddess, "now then do we fulfill the whole duty of man. Having earned our bread by the sweat of our brow, we may eat, drink, and be merry, for to-morrow—"

"For to-morrow," reads the Scribe from a scrap of the Norfolk *Day Book* that is doing temporary duty as a napkin, "a lower temperature over the Atlantic coast, falling barometer, and cloudy with rain areas."

"I never encounter an episode like this," goes on our philosopher, "without recalling dear delightful George Arnold—may his memory be ever green and perennial—the choicest spirit in the annals of Bohemia, who in a moment like this, embodied the whole creed of the fraternity in a few glowing lines. The moment is propitious, and I feel the spirit of that incomparable soul upon me.

> "Here
> With my beer
> I sit,
> While golden moments flit;
> Alas!
> They pass
> Unheeded by;
> And, as they fly,

I,
Being dry,
Sit, idly sipping here
My beer.

"Oh, finer far
Than fame or riches are
The graceful smoke-wreaths
Of this free cigar !
Why
Should I
Weep, wail, or sigh?

"What if luck has passed me by?
What if my hopes are dead—
My pleasures fled?
Have I not still
My fill
Of right good cheer—
Cigars and beer?

" Go, whining youth,
Forsooth !
Go weep and wail,
Sigh and grow pale,
Weave melancholy rhymes
On the old times,
Whose joys, like shadowy ghosts, appear.

"Gold is dross—
Love is loss—

So if I gulp my sorrows down,
    Or see them drown
In foamy draughts of old nut-brown,
    Then do I wear the crown,
    Without the cross !"

"Let us return thanks that your friend Arnold is not here," says the general. "I have been counting the bottles, and I find there is but one apiece. I don't know what the late Mr. Arnold would have considered a *quantum sufficit*, but I don't believe I could witness my sorrows drown in foamy draughts of *one* nut-brown."

"And I don't agree with George Arnold at all," interposes the maiden in pink. "I am afraid he was altogether a fatalist. I rather prefer the ring of Longfellow's lines that teach a creed especially fitted for such dreamers as I am afraid you all are. Do you remember them?"

"I do," says Jack, as he reaches for a deviled crab. "'In the world's broad field of battle, in the great barn-yard of life, be not like dumb-driven Bantams ; be a Shanghai in the strife.' I imagine that Arnold was not much of a Shanghai."

"Jack is right," says Dora. "Won't somebody reach me a pickle?—I think if I were a man—which, thank Heaven, I am not—I would be—no, the pickles !—I would be something more—thank you

—be something more than—" here the white teeth of the goddess shut down fiercely on the green condiment—"an artist or a poet. Oh, how I detest—"

"What, pickles?"

"No, poets. Such as George Arnold, for instance, who imagine that summer holidays have no end, and that the whole aim of existence is smoke and foam. Do you remember the 'Jester's Plea'?"

"Don't I!" says Jack. "Ah, Byron was a man after my own heart.

> "'The world's a merry wench, akin
>   To all that's frail and frightful;
> The world's as ugly—aye, as sin,
>   And nearly as delightful!
> The world's a merry world (*pro tem*),
>   And some are gay, and therefore
> It pleases them, but some condemn
>   The world they do not care for.'"

"Ah, yes," says she, "but I believe Mr. Locker—not Lord Byron, Jack, if you please—had a better grace than to stop with a single stanza. Shall I go on?

> "'The time for pen and sword was when
>   My "ladye fayre" for pity
> Could tend her wounded knight, and then
>   Be tender at his ditty.

Some ladies now make pretty songs,
  And some make pretty nurses ;
Some men are great at righting wrongs,
  And some at writing verses.'"

" Jack is so fond of Locker, hadn't we better give
him another verse?" says Sid, sincerely grateful for
the diversion. " Say this for instance—

"' When Wisdom halts, I humbly try
    To make the most of Folly.
If Pallas be unwilling, I
    Prefer to flirt with Polly ;
To quit the goddess for the maid
    Seems low in lofty musers ;
But Pallas is a lofty jade—
    And beggars can't be choosers.' "

" And speaking of poetry," remarks the general,
after the laugh over Jack's discomfiture had sub-
sided, and Dora, having determined never again to
measure swords with Sid, had recovered from her
confusion, " And speaking of poetry, I wonder
who could have left these lines on my dressing-
case at the hotel. You see my room is next to
Dora's, and some popinjay slipped in while we
were at breakfast, and, I presume, mistaking my
room for hers, left me this tender token of his affection. Thucydides, my friend, I have mislaid my
glasses; will you be so kind as to translate it for me?"

It must have been a stray sunbeam that at this moment, breaking the barrier of the cedars, fell softly upon the garments of the goddess, and reflected their hue upon the countenance of Jack, tinging in their course the cheeks of the divinity herself, who would have arrested the tell-tale lines in their passage had not Sid interposed his long arm and caught them from the general's grasp ere they were scarce rescued from the depths of his pocket.

" These touching lines," said he with a critical air, "were evidently composed under a pressure of emotion.   They are evidently iambics with a trochaic measure.   They don't always scan perfectly, but then perhaps that is excusable.   I imagine the emotion was paroxysmal, superinduced by a rush of brains to the head.   It occurs sometimes to young and very gushing souls, who— But I observe a grave error in their construction that I will endeavor to correct as I read them.   I am always happy to aid struggling genius.

" ' To Dora.

" ' When the moonlight is beaming,
And tipping the waves,
And wavelets are moaning
O'er numberless graves—

> When the breezes are wafting
>> Perfumes of the sea,
> I lounge on the ramparts,
>> And think, love, of thee.
>
> Sing a-too-ral, li-loo-ral, li-loo-ral, li-lay,
> Sing a-too-ral, li-loo-ral, li-loo-ral, li-lay, etc., etc., etc.'

"Of course you understand the chorus is my own. No well-considered poem of this nature is perfect without a chorus. Now, the next verse calls for improvements. There are lamentable oversights that induce me to wonder what the poet could have been thinking of. Jack, my boy, don't fidget so! When my mind is pinned down to poesy I really cannot bear to be diverted by such antics as those. This is not a minstrel show, you know.

> "'When the sea-gulls are calling
>> In shrill, piercing hoots
> (*And the sand-crabs are crawling*
>> *Down into my boots*),
> When the ship-lights are twinkling
>> Far, far out at sea,
> I lounge on the ramparts,
>> And dream, love, of thee.
>
> Sing a-too-ral, li-loo-ral, li-loo-ral, li-*lee*, etc., etc., etc.'

"Now what could be more exquisite than that? Here we enable Miss Dora to comprehend the precise situation, and the difficulties under which the

poet labored. How much better than his own careless lines ! You see, after the young man had told
her about the sea-gulls calling, etc., etc., he goes
on to say that sundry other sea-fowl are '*bawling
from watery coots.*' Now, in the first place, birds
don't 'bawl,' and ' watery coots ' are altogether too
damp for anything but oysters and terrapins. Let
us go on to the next verse, which I find I must re-
construct altogether. There are brilliant possibilities in this poem, which I am surprised should not
have attracted the poet's attention.

> "'A beam from thy window
>   Comes soft thro' the trees
> (*And those beggarly crabs
>   Are climbing my knees*).
> I waft thee a kiss, love
>   (*Great Heavens ! there's a bite !
> Excuse me a moment
>   While I go for a light*).'

" Here you see Miss Dora is enabled to follow the
poem through the whole process of its incubation.
She sees her admirer sitting on the ramparts, buried
in thought, with his eyes far out at sea, catching
now and then a sound of bawling birds (and now
and then a flea). The ship-lights attract his attention; he hears a sea-gull calling to its mate, and
balmy breezes bring perfumes from the flats at

Sewall's Point. He is bathed in the effulgence of
the moonlight and enwrapped in the embrace of
the amatory muse. The goddess woos him to tender verse and leads him to divine pastures and bids
him browse to his heart's content. But soft! what
light through yonder window breaks? Is it the
east, and is Dora the sun? Well, no—it is a kero-
sene lamp from the hotel, and Dora is about to
take down her back hair and retire for the night,
utterly oblivious of the fact that her admirer is
spooning out there in the dampness. Just then he
is diverted by the episode of the sand-crabs, and
proceeds to investigate by the glare of a lucifer
match. The whole scene passes before her like a
glowing panorama—the moonlight, the birds, the
ship-lights, and the crabs. What could be more delightful! But I digress. The next stanza is a perfect gem. It is—"

"Now, really, Mr. Thucy, I cannot permit this
nonsense to go any further," interrupts the fair
Dora. "Not that I have any idea of the identity
of the poet! ["Oh, no!" resounds from all sides—
"to be sure not!"] but I presume he couldn't help
putting his feelings on paper, and I have no doubt
the verses are very good of their kind. Who could
it have been, I wonder? Can you imagine, Mr.
Longmeter?"

8

"Saul," remarks that worthy in the calmest and most deliberate of tones, "I find by this copy of the *Virginian* that the boat from Elizabeth City leaves at five o'clock A.M. If we are going, there are preparations to make, and unless I am much mistaken there is a storm coming up from the Capes. What were you asking me, Miss Dora? Oh! the verses? Upon my word, I haven't an idea. What are you all laughing at? Sid, I thought I understood you to say this was not a minstrel performance?"

"Nor is it," says the Pharisee—"nor is it, my boy. The storm may overtake us before we can reach town, and storms in this latitude are too attentive, by half. Let us leave the cedars behind us, with the cares that infest the day, while we pick up our feet like the Arabs, and silently steal away. Let the Scribe record in the minutes that we leave here in the morning for the Lower Elizabeth and the Lake of the Dismal Swamp."

Obediently,

SAUL WRIGHT.

VII.

Aus Nacht, Durch Liebe, Zu Licht.

Elizabeth City, N. C.,
September 3, 18—.

We have passed through the valley of the shadow of death. We have glided through a corner of the delightful kingdom. We have discerned entrances to the infernal regions. We have caught glimpses of Paradise. We have discovered the gloom and the darkness of desolation, and discerned the splendor of luxuriance. What a strange anomaly is the Dismal Swamp! We are disappointed—and delighted. We had expected the superlative of waste, desolation, and horror, and the half had not been told us. We had anticipated a dismal swamp, and found delightful meadows.

We had steamed slowly up the picturesque Elizabeth, where luxuriant verdure comes down to the river side, and teeming fields were merry with the hum of the harvest ; where glorious landscapes of mead and meadow stretched out without limit, and magnificent woodlands swelled and rolled away to the foot of mounting hills. We had glided through transparent depths where water-grasses tickled the ribs of our sturdy little steamer, and wound in and out a meadowy passage where land and river were indivisible. Now we are surrounded by towering trees, where vines interlace, and creepers mount, and tendrilous moss hangs in graceful festoons, and strange birds are whistling stranger songs. Here are the bay and the myrtle, the juniper and the cypress, and a tangled drapery veils the mysteries beyond. Now we shoot from delightful shade to the glare of sunlight and a fair opening, where fields of grain are attended by busy harvesters, and rustic cottages are set on shady knolls, and wind in and out from light to shadow and from gloom to glare. Now we enter a long, narrow stretch, where dismantled trees are packed like masts at the wharves of a seaport, and charred trunks are planted in blackened soil, and again we dart out into fields of luxuriant undergrowth. And this is the Dismal Swamp.

Our Pharisee is in his element, our artist in raptures, and our divinity divine. The poet lounges by her side; the hour is propitious and the air infectious with harmony. Suddenly the silence is broken as a clear contralto rings out on the startled air, and, as if waiting the summons, four ringing voices take up the refrain :

'They made her a grave too cold and damp
　For a heart so loving and true ;
She has gone to the Lake of the Dismal Swamp
Where all night long, by a fire-fly lamp,
　She paddles her white canoe.

" Her fire-fly lamp I soon shall see—
　Her paddle I soon shall hear ;
Long, long, and loving our lives shall be ;
I'll hide the maid in a cypress-tree
　When the footstep of Death is near."

"I regret," said the general, "that we shall not see the lake. If I remember correctly, it is some four miles to the east of the line of the canal, and is reached by a feeder. I am told that Lake Drummond has a circumference of about twenty miles, a width of seven, and a depth of fifteen feet. A peculiarity about it is its color and its remarkable purity. It resembles strong coffee, or, as coffee is frequently muddy, say rather like clear Cognac, and so fresh and pleasant is it to the taste that it has become an article of commerce, its remarkable purity commending it as excellent for long sea voyages."

" And it was also at the lake where the tragedy of Moore's lines was supposed to have been enacted," remarks Sid. "It is upon the whole a pleasing legend, based upon the phenomenon of the *ignis-fatuus*, that is remarkably addicted to frequenting this locality. I wonder in which of these huge cypresses that amphibious maid is secreted. What a splendid field for the 'rhumatiz,' by the way! I wonder if, during her long residence here, she has discovered a remedy for the chills and fever. What a glittering opportunity she has to become a benefactress."

And again the voices ring out o'er the summer morning, and are echoed from the forest:

> "Away to the Dismal Swamp he speeds;
>   His path was rugged and sore,
>   Thro' tangled juniper, beds of reeds,
>   And many a fen where the serpent feeds
>   And man never trod before.

> "And when on the ground he sank to sleep—
>   If slumber his eyelids knew—
>   He lay where the deadly vine doth weep
>   Its venomous tear, and nightly steep
>   The flesh with blistering dew."

Onward we push through the narrow water-way, and the smiling meadows are left behind, and dark, slimy pools over whose green filmy surfaces hang buzzing gnats, and loathsome nondescripts peer out upon us from either side. Here strange contorted roots, and gnarled stumps, and grotesque trunks lift up from stagnant depths, and over fallen logs strange reptiles creep, and black, hideous turtles lift their wriggling heads, and a water-snake squirms lazily in and out among them. Here is a gum-tree from whose upper branches a "possum" hangs by his clinging tail, and calls shrilly to the echoes. Again the voices :

> "He saw the lake, and a meteor bright
>   Quick over its surface played.
> 'Oh, welcome,' he cried, 'my dear one's light!'
> And the dim shores echoed for many a night
>   The name of the death-cold maid."

"Ugh!" shouts the lady of our party, "what horrid creatures are the insects of this dismal place! I have killed one that I would like to have stuffed and mounted on a pedestal. And I really believe we have run into a swarm that numbers millions. Suppose we postpone the rest of the song until evening. What are we to do? Why, they are perfectly awful. They are unendurable, maddening!"

It was certainly the most remarkable exhibition of mosquito growth we had ever encountered. They came by regiments and corps and armies; they were voiceless, but noisy because of their multitude, and ye gods! how they bit. We might

have descended to the cabin, but the cabin was
stifling, and the dampness penetrated its windows,
and the odor of cookery was intolerable. So we
compromise the situation by muffling our heads in
veils and handkerchiefs, and carry on an unsatis-
factory conversation in stifled tones that is soon
abandoned for the silence of profundity, except as
occasional expletives are forced from muffled lips
by some unusually persistent bloodthirsty mite.
Sid and I threw ourselves on a pile of bags and
ropes on the after-deck; the hum of the mosquitoes
grew fainter and fainter, the swashing of the waves
as they washed against the sides of the boat grew
duller and lighter, the drowsiness of the noonday
pressed down upon our eyelids, and we slept.

I was roaming the depths of the Dismal Swamp,
pursuing white ladies in birch canoes, and following meteor sparks into slimy pools, where turtles
and snakes were hanging by their tails to dripping
gum-trees, and having an uncommonly damp time
of it, when a punch in the ribs aroused me, and
I beheld Sid bending over my pillow of rope, and
in queer pantomime imposing the silence of death.
Then I heard voices behind us : voices of entreaty
and of petulance ; persuasive accents and laughing,
teasing replies ; muffled voices that came through
thicknesses of veils and handkerchiefs ; absurd, pre-

posterous voices that sounded as dismal as the swamps. We feigned the deepest slumber. I am not sure but we snored occasionally, but we listened.

"Dora," whispered the sharp, nervous voice of the troubadour, "do you remember the verses that Sid made so much sport of yesterday at Brambleton ?"

"I should think I had good reasons to," responds Dora, through the folds of her veil. "I was never so mortified in my life. No, never! and I am not going to say 'hardly ever,' either—ugh! there's a mosquito inside my glove! No, never."

"But, Dora, did you imagine who wrote them ?"

"Do you think I am such a goose as to imagine there is another man in all the world who would write such insipid nonsense? Ouch! there's a bite on my ear! Why can't you drive them away? And to think of your putting them on papa's dressing-case !"

"But, Dora, they are not so very bad, you know, if you could only see them," pleaded Jack.

"What, the mosquitoes ?"

"No, the verses, I mean. Confound that big fellow! I believe he has gone up my coat-sleeve! No, I mean the verses."

"The verses gone up your coat-sleeve, Jack ?"

"No, of course not, the mosquitoes. They are right good, I think. Won't you let me read them to you, Dora?"

"What in the world are you talking about? Is it the mosquitoes that are right good, or the verses that bite? How you do mix things up. Oh! there's one on my hand! Kill him, quick! But you needn't hold my hand; he isn't coming back again."

"But, Dora, don't you know the verses were true? I meant every word of it."

"Did you, really? Why, I thought it was all Mr. Thucy's nonsense. Did the sand-crabs really plague you, and did you light a match to find them? What fun it must have been."

"Sand-crabs be blowed! Of course that was Sid's nonsense. I will pay him for it, too, some day. But don't you know how the verses ended? Don't you remember I said—Great Cæsar, there's a wasp!"

"No, did you? I didn't hear them read properly, you know, but I don't know that I ever heard of wasps flying about in the moonlight. There, quick, Jack! Don't you see that swarm right over my head?"

"There, they're gone now. But you know I said something about thinking of thee. And you know

I told you the other evening that I had lost my heart to some one, and you said—Holy Moses! he's stung me on the thumb! There, I've got him."

"Why, Jack, I never said anything of the kind."

"I didn't mean that you said that ; of course you didn't. But you said, 'Where did you lose it?' and I said I would tell you some time, and—Dora, what are you laughing at?"

"Why, you silly fellow, I can't tell for the life of me what you are talking about. First you say I said something about Moses and a wasp, and then you said you'd got him, and then you say I didn't say that, but that I did say that you'd lost him. Are you talking about wasps, Jack, or what?"

"May his Infernal Highness take all the wasps and mosquitoes and the Dismal Swamp into the bargain! Dora, I couldn't help saying it. Pardon me, won't you? And won't you let me show them to you?"

"Jack, if you show me a wasp, I'll scream, and I'll never forgive you, and I'll—"

"But I am not going to show you any wasps. I mean the verses. That is, I mean that I don't mean that I'm going to show you any verses— I mean any wasps. Oh, what the devil do I mean?"

"I am sure I haven't any idea what you *do* mean,

Jack, only you are getting terribly excited over something. Between the verses and the wasps and the mosquitoes, I am so awfully confused that I have lost all track of what you commenced to tell me about. Suppose you commence all over again ?"

" But I am not going to commence all over again. After struggling over the ground so far I am not going to lose the benefit of it. But I said in the verses that Sid didn't read that—there's a devil's darning-needle right on your shoulder ! quick !"

"Then I'm glad that he didn't read it. How in the world could you have seen a darning-needle in my room when you were away out on the ramparts ?"

"Oh, pshaw ! I didn't say that in the verses, you ninny. I said—"

"Jack, I am not a ninny, and I'm not going to be called names either. You said that you said in the verses that there was a darning-needle on my shoulder."

"But there was one there a moment ago, and I frightened him off. Why won't you let me tell you what I mean ?"

"Upon my word I do wish I knew what you do mean. You have been talking about Moses and Cæsar and wasps and darning-needles and— Jack,

I am going down into the cabin. I cannot stand this any longer."

"But hold on, Dora, don't go just yet. I just want to tell you that I don't care for anybody in the world but—shoo! plague take the mosquitoes, shoo! shoo!—that I don't care for anybody in the world but—sh-h-h-oo—they are thicker now than ever—for anybody in the world but—shoo-oo-oo!—"

"Jack, are you crazy? If you don't care for anything in the world but *shoes* I don't know why you need to shout it out in that insane manner. Is that what you wanted to tell me? But I never buy my own shoes. Papa always buys them. You must speak to papa."

"*May* I speak to papa? Is that what you mean, Dora? Oh, bless you, my darling! You don't know how I love you!—shoo! shoo!—You don't know how happy you make me!"

"Mr. Longmeter, I am surprised! Do you really mean to say that you have been making love to me all this time? Did I ever encourage you in any such madness? What *have* I done to make you tell me that? You know that I don't love you. I don't love anybody, and I didn't ask you to love me, and I didn't want you to write verses about me, and—quick, Jack, there's a big hornet on my veil! Thank you. Now you foolish fellow, let's go down in the cabin, and if you ever talk such nonsense again I shall cut your acquaintance."

"But, Dora, let me—"

"Not another word, sir, if you want me to be your friend. It can never be, Jack, so don't think of it any more. You don't know how sorry you make me to have to tell you. And Jack—I'd—I'd rather you wouldn't call me *Dora*. Nobody but papa does that, you see—and—you may call me anything else, but—but—that sounds too familiar. Don't you think so? For believe me, Jack, I don't want to offend you, but it can never be. I can't tell you why, but it can never—never—never be. Now come let's go down in the cabin."

"But Do— I mean Miss Dora—I may call you Miss Dora, mayn't I?—you won't tell the rest of them about this, will you? You know they would chaff me so, and it is bad enough as it is."

"No, Jack—I mean Mr. Longmeter—I will promise not to breathe it to a soul, if you'll promise to never do so again. But remember, sir, the very first time—" and two muffled heads disappear down the gangway.

"What could have possessed Jack to make such an exhibition of himself?" said Sid, after we had recovered from the recoil consequent upon the explosion of laughter that had been accumulating

until we had been brought to the verge of suffoca-
tion. "If that interview had continued another
moment I should have strangled. As it was, it was
Jack who was strangled. By Jove! how admirably
she did it! What a beautiful guard she kept!
What a splendid parry! Her high tierce was admirable—her *moulinets* wonderful—her thrusts superb! She's a perfect master of fence, my boy,
an opponent that I shouldn't care to tackle, unless
I was sure of my cause. As for Jack, the blunder-
ing dunce, what right had he to imagine for a moment that she was the kind of a bird to be caught
with chaff? But that lesson won't do him a par-
ticle of good, you know. I don't really believe it
will last him over night. Saul, we must clinch that
nail ourselves. I won't have her worried again by
that wretched Jack."

Why in the world should it concern him, I wonder? Why should that incorrigible Pharisee interfere between Jack and his little amusements? Why
should Sid worry himself over a woman—a woman
in pink—a woman from Culpepper—who dresses in
pink, you remember, because she would be a fright
in white, and who, from the misfortune of sex, cannot say anything worth remembering? *Tempora
mutantur, etc., etc., etc.*

And still we drift onward. Huge cypress trees,

hung with festoons of parasitic moss, over-arch our watery progress. Gnarled vines in fantastic tangles, rank underbrush, stunted pines, huge trunks —charred, blackened, and smouldering with hidden fire, form the motive for the scene that surrounds us. Now and then an opening, where dusky groups of negroes lounge about what may be saw-mills or crematory furnaces or haunted hamlets. One can conceive anything possible in the Dismal Swamp. Here and there a mass of smoking timber, which a rain-fall of a week has failed to quench; a space cleared by the flames; an inland oasis, rich and smiling with tropical verdure; and then, vast matted walls of reeds shut in the scene, and we drift through thickets of juniper, green brier, and cypress. We are sailing the Stygian stream—lost souls are wandering about us—filmy ghosts flit in and out the tangled hedges—sleep and death have their abode beyond and beneath— above is the infinite, the vast, the unknowable. Here, indeed,

> ". . . the deadly vine doth weep
> Its venomous tears, and nightly steep
> The flesh with blistering dew."

Now lazy, loathsome buzzards, with rushing wings, drop from some perch above us, and sail lazily away to brood over the wrongs of their disturbance ; a rattling coppersnake glides from a rotting log, and shining lizards dart in and out the cane-brakes. Here, the very earth is burning with unquenchable fires ; hot flames dart out from red-hot beds of peat, and we breathe the smoke from the Plutonian regions. Ha ! ha ! a light, an opening—the broad glare of day—the sun—the free air —and we glide into freedom. Out of the jaws of death ! out from the mouth of hell ! out of the Dismal Swamp.

If I were called upon to decide between the cabin and the deck of this remarkable craft, I am not at all sure how I should award the preference. If we had been entomologists on a skirmishing tour for rare specimens, I presume we should have found the deck a perfect elysium, or had a vapor-bath been prescribed by our medical attendant, the cabin would have afforded a brilliant opportunity. But being merely tourists, with a slight regard for the preservation of our moral and physical temper, either part of the boat was equally execrable. However, we did manage to remain below long enough to absorb a limited quantity of the most wretched atoms of fish, flesh, and fowl imaginable, prepared by a culinary process the most villainous known to history.

9

"My dear Angelo," remarked the General, as he transferred a morsel of oleaginous matter from his plate to that of the artist, "I am reaching the sere and yellow leaf, where my eyes are unable to distinguish between the hoof of the steer and the bifurcated pedal extremity of the swine. Will you be kind enough to analyze this substance and enlighten me as to its identity?"

"With but a limited knowledge of chemicals," responds Dick, after a careful prodding of his fork, "I confess myself unworthy of the flattering distinction you have conferred upon me. Had the cook exercised a trifle more care in removing the bristles he might have imposed it upon us for terrapin. As it is, the flesh is apparently the flesh of Jacob, but the hair is the hair of Esau."

"I am inclined to think it a bit of fricasseed watermelon," remarked Jack, after an investigation, "and I should imagine from the odor it had been smothered in garlic."

"Oh! thank you," and the General emptied the balance of his plate through the cabin window. "I was fearful that I had been consuming a morsel of 'the death-cold maid.' I wonder if that unhappy youth ever recovered her remains? I shall decline fish, I think, until we are clear away from this melancholy spot."

"He never recovered them, General," says Sid.
"I am assured upon the best authority that on one
dark, tempestuous occasion he encountered her
ghost in the light canoe, and implored her in tearful accents to permit him to read her the thrilling
lines we howled an hour ago," and the Pharisee
proceeds to open a watermelon and distribute its
scarlet segments around the board.

"And what did she say?" inquires Dora, as she
snaps a seed across the table to Jack.

"What did she say? Oh, she said—Great Cæsar! there's a wasp!"

"What a remark for a ghost to make in a dark,
tempestuous night!" laughs the goddess, as she
shoots a puzzled look of inquiry over at Jack. "I
should have thought he would have fled the spot."

"Oh, no, indeed!" says Sid. "Faint heart ne'er
won fair lady, you know. He merely insisted upon
reading her the verses ; nay, he implored her, on
his bended knees, although, as I have said, the
night was awfully unpleasant, and his boat was
leaking."

"And what response did she make to his im-
portunities?" inquired Dora, a little desirous of
learning the drift of the story, and altogether fearful of the answer.

"What did she say? Well, you see as he insisted

upon an answer, she said—what *did* she. say, Saul,
by the way? I am afraid I have forgotten."

"She said—Holy Moses! he's bit me on the
thumb!" responds the Scribe, obediently.

"Why, she never said anything of the kind,"
goes on the remorseless wretch, as the face of the
goddess took on the hue of the melon she was pick-
ing. "She said that he said that she said—no, I
mean that he said the verses—I mean the wasp—
oh, what the devil do I mean!" he shouted as Jack
went under the table in search of his knife, and
Dora fled the cabin with precipitation and ringing
laughter, in which Sid participated.

"Bless my heart!" says the General, "what is it
all about? Jack, my friend, what are you doing
under the table?"

"He's in love with his shoes," explains Sid.
"You have no conception of the limits of Jack's
eccentricity, my dear General ; he is a mystery to
his dearest friends. I have an idea, to be sure, regarding the cause of his present madness, but I
wouldn't mention it for worlds—you know you fellows would chaff him so. Jack, my boy, come out
from under the table. You are forgiven if you'll
promise to never do so again. But remember, sir,
the very first time—General, we are clear of the
Dismal Swamp, and plowing the waters of the

Pasquotank.   What do you say to an hour of penny-ante?"

And thus we invade North Carolina.

Tar-dily,

SAUL WRIGHT.

VIII.

A Nocturne in Ultramarine.

WELDON, N. C., September 10, 18—.

BEFORE leaving Norfolk, we inquired of a chance acquaintance regarding the characteristics of Eastern North Carolina. "If you are in search of the beautiful or the picturesque, in nature or humanity," said he, "you will likely be disappointed." He was right in the abstract. "A vast stretch of water," he went on, in comprehensive summary, "ragged with indentations, and huge, fine forests, reaching through a swampy section, sparsely populated, little improved, and wholly wretched." We note exceptions in the concrete. We are indisposed to be critical, being enthusiastic pilgrims leisurely roving without a commission, and content to accept what the gods provide. How we were transported from Elizabeth to Edenton, where the boisterous Chowan rolls down to the Albemarle; how we crossed to Plymouth, where the Roanoke makes into the piney forests; how we skirted the waters of Pamlico from Hatteras to Lookout, and met the white waters of the Neuse

at Newberne, I have really forgotten. Was it by
puffing steamer with wheezy hitches and turns, or
lazy lugger that drifted here and there at the
caprice of the lazier winds, or tidy yacht with full
sail and spanking boom, that swept boldly in and
out the watery paths, or a combination of all? I
haven't the slightest conception. It is of little consequence. You cannot expect the Scribe of a summer's pilgrimage, you know, to descend to petty
details.

I recall a quiet morning when we stole out of
the Pasquotank, and followed the ragged outlines
of Currituck and Perquimans, where pine forests
came down to the water's edge, and a long sandy
beach-line shut out the ocean. I recall an hour
when the mid-day breeze curled the broad bosom
of the Albemarle and white-capped waves danced
in fantastic glee, and fierce gulls and fish-hawks cir-
cled and sailed with shrill, piercing cries; and
then we drifted languidly into the mouth of the
black Chowan, where white smoke curled up from
brown cottages, and dusky fishermen were hauling
overflowing seines, and a cool wooded point echoed
with shouts of merry woodmen, as, with the red
sun sinking in a haze of golden glory, we made
into a delightful bay and were at anchor. I am
reminded of a charming little seaport, where ven-

erable mansions were hid among venerable groves, and an aged church stood, ivy-covered and solemn, in the midst of moss-grown tombs and drooping willows, like Niobe—all tears ; of a village green that sloped down to the brink of the river, and picturesque villas and broad estates that bordered the environs of Edenton.

There came a day when we left Roanoke Island and Manteo on our quarter, and dashed boldly into Pamlico Sound, where we beat and tacked and scampered before a stiff wind, and laughed at the flying scuds, and made sport of a family of Mother Cary's chickens, that hooted and haunted our wake, and watched dark, gloomy clouds piling in huge, forbidding mountains, angry waves that hurled themselves against our sides, and drenched us with salt, generous spray, and the lightning flashed, the thunder rolled and tumbled, the rains descended and the floods came, and we welcomed the spires of Newberne as the most cherished friends of a lifetime. There were mornings of delightful banter and small-talk, noons of subtle and erudite argument, and evenings of song. We were genial and merry, sullen and sulky by turns, first grave and gay, then lively and serene ; we fished, smoked, read, and chaffed, then smoked and fished again. We wondered what the world was doing in our absence, and sighed to think it might possibly be getting along without us. We breakfasted on fish and crabs, lunched to the accompaniment of shrimps and oysters, and dined upon marine monsters of every conceivable pattern and shape. We woke to dream the hours away, and slept to dream them back. You see it is all a confusing dream at the best, a mingling of facts and fancies, a grand *pasticcio* of a summer's holiday. It is all a delightful memory.

When I wrote you from Old Point that the Culpepper party was a decided acquisition to our number, I had but faint ideas of all that the term has implied. It has become the jolliest fellowship imaginable. So far as the gray old General is concerned, we wonder how we have ever got along without him. From the merry jest to the serious bout of skill we have found him ever ready, eager, and willing. No sport has been too fatiguing, no hour too late for his cheery laugh and hearty aid. When we have become dull and gloomy, when even the irrepressible Pharisee has called a halt, and the poet has reached a period in his memories, then has the brave old veteran thrown himself into the breach, assumed the sway, sat by our side, and talked and smoked the night away, "wept o'er his wounds, or tales of sorrow done; shouldered

his crutch and showed how fields were won." Decidedly, we should never have survived without the
General. And what shall I say of our goddess?
With what fitting words can I convey the gratitude
which four wretched Bohemians, who had projected
a rambling tour to nowhere in particular, feel for
the gracious divinity who has invaded their ranks,
grasped the reins with her own charming hands,
while she directs the course of the pilgrimage, as
they follow willingly, obediently, gratefully, eagerly
in her train? What a stupid, tiresome, wretched,
and altogether pitiful affair it would have been
without her! What excesses we have avoided,
what dreariness evaded, what agreeable limits it
has placed upon our lips, and what delightful sac-
rifices imposed upon our passions! What a perfect, jolly, rollicking time it has been altogether!
Brave, sunny, merry, indulgent little goddess, we
kiss our hands to you.

It is little less than honest candor for me to confess that from the silver-headed General to the
blushing Scribe we have all become rivals for her
gracious favor, and nothing more than candid hon-
esty for me to admit her studied impartiality and
her easy justice. Jack is never reminded of his unfortunate temerity, nor Dick of the abandoned
"effort of his life." The Scribe is made happy by

her sympathy and perfect cordiality of tastes and hobbies, and from her impenetrable armor the cynical shafts of the Pharisee fall shattered and harmless. If I have detected flashing moments when she has permitted her ardent eyes to dwell meltingly upon his, or a quick blush to o'erspread her cheeks at some careless, thoughtless word, that was permitted to pass unrebuked, I have deemed it but the homage we are all compelled to pay to our philosopher, our mentor, and our sage.

Thus does the Scribe condense in a few sweeping paragraphs the delightful progress of our pilgrimage.

We are loath to leave the sea-coast. For the better part of a month our days have been glad dened by the sight of the vast, illimitable blue above and around us, and our nights have been lulled by the ever-breaking, washing, moaning waves. They have come to be a part of our pilgrimage. We look upon them as old and familiar friends. They have been ever constant, true, and abiding ; they will be to us through the balance of our earthly pilgrimage an endearing memory.

It was generally agreed that our last evening at Newberne should be devoted to the ocean and a final adieu to Father Neptune. The evening was irreproachable ; the air soft and balmy as the air of Paradise; the water smooth and obedient, and above us hung the full, round, laughing moon, who sent her beams to dance on the tips of the wavelets and mellow the night with liquid splendor. We pulled out to the mouth of the dreamy Neuse, drifted lazily about at the caprice of the foolish breezes, and sailed through a silver sea to the shores of Bœetia. What preposterous yarns and nonsensical stories were told; what absurd songs and choruses awoke the shores of old Pamlico; what outrageous puns were perpetrated, and what demoniac peals of laughter broke the stillness of the night, as that rakish little center-board with its merry cargo, rambled aimlessly and carelessly on the brow of the astonished waters. It was a night made up of parodies and puns, and similes that were far-fetched, and *double-entendres* that were obscure, and a tithe of its proceedings, if preserved —which, thank Heaven, they are not—would have founded the fortune of an enterprising and wholly unprincipled paragrapher of the period, or restored the waning fortunes of a negro-minstrel troupe.

Suddenly a shrill cry pierces the startled night as a phantom craft with huge black sail stands dimly away to the leeward. As we had drifted leisurely in toward the shore all unconscious of our course, it had rapidly swept down upon us, and tacking suddenly, had appeared as though let down from the heavens by some invisible hand.

"Ship ahoy!"

"Ship ahoy yourself! *Qui vive?*" shouts Sid through a roll of music which has become an impromptu speaking-trumpet. "That must be the *Flying Dutchman*," he remarks *sotto voce.*

"What boat is that?" comes in gruff tones over the water.

"Her Majesty's ship *Pinafore!*"

"Who commands her?"

"A clerk from the Navy Department."

"Who have you got aboard?"

"The Queen of Bohemia and her court."

"Where are you bound?"

"We are on our way to the court of Neptune, *pour prendre congé.*"

"On yer way to court! I reckon it will be to ther perlice court—you hear *me?* But what are yer doin' in thar?"

"We have lost our reckoning—been blown out of our course—lost our compass overboard, and the pilot's down with the chills."

"Well, we've got a shot-gun out here, and plenty of buck-shot, and if yer don't make yerself scarce, we're going to use it."

"This is undoubtedly an example of the Yazoo

plan," says Sid to his crew. " Shall we withdraw
from the canvas ? Never !" Then in herculean
tones, " Refrain, audacious tar, your suit from
pressing. Remember whom you are, and whom
addressing. We are corsairs on a midnight prowl."

" Well, I thought so. But yer better prowl out'er
thar—you hear me ? You're a nice sailor, *you* are !"

I admit it was inexcusable—perfectly unpardonable—but we recalled the fact that we were off the
barbarous coast of North Carolina, and as Dora
remarked in whispered accents, " Sing, hey, the
thoughtful sailor that you are," five lusty voices
took up the refrain with a terminal that was deep,
guttural, and excruciating :

> " The merry, merry maiden, the merry, merry maiden,
>   The merry, merry ma-a-de-en,
>   And the
>   TAR—"

" What are yer howling about ?" was the response
to this musical effort. " We ain't going fur to scut-
tle yer. What's yer name, boss—you feller that's
making so much noise ?"

" My name is Norval ; on the Gramp—" whispered Dora.

" What did yer soy ?"

" Now see here, my Christian friend," responds

Sid, and nearly splits his throat in the effort, "we are out here on a lark, and we don't care to be disturbed. I haven't any cards with me, but my name is *Corcoran*, and I command the *Pinafore*."

"Oh, Pinnerfore be d—d! We don't keer what yer command—only if yer don't get outside of that ere seine I'll run yer all through with a marline-spike! You hear *me!*"

Shades of Neptune and all the naiads defend us! The Queen of Bohemia and five of her most trusty subjects to be run through with a marline-spike! Skewered like so many herrings—ugh! The picture was not a delightful one. We were in no particular haste, but we got outside of that seine. We stood not upon the order of our going, but went at once. With no means of verifying the matter, we feel convinced that that amphibious monster was fully capable of carrying that strange threat into execution. We had determined from the setting out of our pilgrimage that we would set Fate at defiance, and in no manner to interfere with any designs which that mythological spinster might be pleased to have upon us. We had braved the dangers of sea and land ; we had looked death and heil in the face ; we had stood on the verge of annihilation and faltered not. But to be confronted with the horror of journeying into the great hereafter on the point of a marline-spike, for all we knew to the contrary, to spend all eternity in that embarrassing condition, was too much for us. Great heavens! what a mortifying termination to a summer's pilgrimage.

Oh, yes! we got out of "that ere seine." In fact how did we get into it? It is among the inscrutable mysteries of existence that will never be explained this side the grave. We made particularly lively tracks from that vicinity. The prow of our gondola was turned toward the west, the sails were set to catch every square inch of a favoring breeze. We slipped, we slid, we gloomed, we glanced, among the skimming swallows; we made the netted moonbeams dance against the sandy shallows. We hummed, we boomed, we blew, we flew, we chased the skipping shadows. We hurried by the river's mouth, and skurried by the meadows. In fact, without expatiating further on the subject, we made about eighty knots an hour toward Newberne. There was a painful lull in the conversation. A silence had descended like a mantle and enwrapped us. There was nothing to be said that had not been said already. We felt that we were looking our last, for a season at least, upon the grand old ocean, and we regretted the parting. We tied up to a dreamy old wharf, just as the smallest of the small hours tolled from a neighboring belfry, and in painful silence sought our abiding place. Six hours later, we had boarded the train, and were speeding away from Newberne.

*   *   *   *   *   *

The scenery between Newberne and Goldsboro and beyond is not to that degree enchanting as to absorb the gaze, nor is the speed of the train so terrific as to disquiet the nerves, or at all interfere in the study of nature in repose. It is not a lightning train. I imagine a streak of lightning would have been soothed gently and calmly to sleep had it attempted to accompany the train that rattled us along through the piney swamps of North Carolina. It was fortunate that our plans had not contemplated haste in the progress of our pilgrimage, else we should have been sorely tempted to have got out and walked to Goldsboro. Yet one had such a delightful feeling of security in the thought that nothing less than a sudden cessation of the earth's motion on its axis can ever throw a North Carolinian railway-train from its track. It seemed at first as though a possible danger lurked in the haunting idea of a collision. Not that there existed a possibility of our running into anything ahead of us; but it seemed extremely probable that the authorities of the road might send out another

10

train to look for us, in which event we might have
suffered from a diversion in the rear. Nothing of
the kind occurred, however, owing to the fact that
ours was an "accommodation train." It was the
most accommodating train we ever encountered.
It would halt at unassuming stations by the way-
side, where the conductor would get off and stroll
around the little town to drum up passengers; it
would stand by the half hour at strange-looking
water-tanks or beside some poverty-stricken wood-
pile; and again, when we had flattered ourselves
that we were fairly under way, and taking on something that was an apology for speed, some old
woman would shake a rag from some tumble-down
shanty, and we would pull up with a shake, a yank,
and a jerk, and our very obliging conductor would
alight and wander off to the tumble-down, to return in the course of time with a basket of eggs or
a pair of fowls, to be delivered at a similar tumble-
down a mile or so further along.

It was while waiting at one of these deserted
wood-piles for the engineer and fireman to saw and
split a relay of motive power, that a long-legged,
slab-sided native ambled along on the sorriest nag
ever permitted to remain unburied, and after an
extended confab with our conductor, tied the animal aforesaid to a concentric rail fence by the side

of the wood-pile, threw his saddle-bags across his arm, and boarded the train. He was a godsend to our lonely party. We welcomed him to our arms, and would have pressed him to our hearts with gratitude, but for the fear he would have been offended. He didn't look like a man who needed any pressing, but who would have been exceedingly grateful for a trifle of expansion. With that end in view we invited him to partake of our lunch, and regretted it a moment later. The perceptible effect of our sacrifice was to unhinge the tongue of that unhappy man, and set it going with a reckless speed that more nearly approached perpetual motion than anything in our experience.

"So you uns are visitin' North Car'lina jist for pleasure," said our new friend. "Wa'll now it's a right smart kintry you bet! Never seed anything ekul to it afore, I reckon, did ye? Did yer notice the craps down below? The craps are looking poorly jist now, but yer o'r't to seen 'em a month ago. Why, stranger, we raises craps in North Car'lina that beats the world, I reckon! Oh, I tell yer, we uns is right smart farmers. I done got an inion patch on my place, stranger, that'd make yer eyes water to look at 'um. I done got hogs as'll weigh two hundred poun'! How's that? Ef yer want to see farmin' as is farmin' yer'v jist kim to the right place fur to see, now you hear *me*. But yit it's nuthin' to what it ware foh the wah !"

"Ah, my friend," inquires the general, "I presume your country was greatly devastated by the ravages of the late unhappy conflict. Doubtless it will be many years before you will wholly recuperate."

"Wall, now, stranger, I don't altogether catch yer meanin'; but if yer go fur to mean that North Car'lina ain't jist the peartest kintry in the *U*-nited States, then I go fur to say yer haven't traveled much, you hear *me*. Yer jist ought fur to see Kurnel Jones's place over in Pitt County, you *had* that. Why, stranger, Kurnel Jones hez raised pertaters that beat the world. Ef yer want to see sweet pertaters as is 'taters, and inions, and guberpeas, yer jist orter go over in Pitt County. Pitt's a right smart county fer guberpeas, but it's nuthin' to what it was foh the wah !"

"I presume it is remarkably healthy around here, is it not?" says Jack.

"Wall, we has right smart chills hereabouts, but we uns don't mind that. I've got 'leven children, stranger, and I'm a young man yit, and they jist has their little chill as reg'lar as clock-work, an' if I duz say it, as shouldn't, there isn't a healthier set er young uns in Lenner County, you hear *me*. My ole 'ooman she's generally down with the jaunders, but she kin hoe her row with any man in this section. Oh, yes, North Car'lina's a mighty healthy country, yer can bet on that, but it's nuthin' to be compared to what it was foh the wah !"

"I am particularly pleased," says the artist, "with your scenery. Nature has been kind to you, and surrounds you with her choicest works. You should be happy, my friend, in the enjoyment of these lovely hills and blooming valleys."

"Oh, yes, we've got right smart hills," responds the native with enthusiasm. "I don't bet much on hills myself ; but my ole 'ooman she ses sometimes, ses she, ' Them hills looks jist ekul to a pictur,' an' cum to look at um, sure enuf they does. Ef yer taken that way, stranger, I kin show yer some hills and rocks and things as 'ud make your mouth water. There's some places along the Noose that I reckon is han'somer than enything in the world. You can stan' on a big high rock down in Lenner County and see all over North Car'lina, I reckon. Oh, yes, we has right smart scenery; but, stranger, yer jest orter seen it foh the wah !"

After passing Goldsboro, where we strike the main line from Wilmington and Charleston, evidences of a higher civilization and a greater prodigality of nature burst suddenly upon us. Teeming

fields from which the yellow-headed wheat is awaiting the harvest, huge corn-fields with their nodding, waving stalks ; here and there a cotton patch
where bursting bolls appear like balls of snow, and
again, vast fields of tobacco where busy pickers
are hurrying about as thick as the leaves on the hill-
sides. Now we dash through thriving villages or
halt in the midst of a busy town, and are off and
away to catch a glimpse of distant hills and winding rivers, or rattle through long stretches of dense
forests, and thunder across broad streams and iron
bridges. Then the shades of night close in; papers,
books, and passing hills and dales are forgotten,
and we drowse to the easy motion of the train.
Suddenly I hear voices beside me, and note a slack-
ening of speed.

"What place mought this be, Masser Sid?"
shouts auntie.

"Weldon, good and faithful servant," I hear Sid
reply. "Thou hast been faithful over a few things;
I will make thee ruler over many. In other words,
auntie, gather up the bundles and wake up your
nephews and niece. We have reached the end of
our day's journey."

Thankfully,

SAUL WRIGHT.

IX.

An Inexcusable Digression.

PETERSBURG, VA.,
September 12, 18—.

I AM not wholly able to explain why we are at Petersburg. Perhaps, however, that simple inability to explain the why and the wherefore of things has been the most delightful part of our wanderings. Since leaving Old Point there has been no controversy concerning our route ; no differences of opinion regarding this stopping-place or the other ; no questioning, and certainly no explanations. We have simply drifted along without much concern as to where we were going, or why we were stopping, or when the journey was to end. Our plans have involved the simplest of geometrical problems. We have let A represent the initial, B the objective point. Query : How shall we get from A to B ? That once decided, we have considered the matter settled, and washed our hands individually and collectively of the whole business of petty details.

Thus it happened that we halted over night at Weldon. Traveling at night had been voted a bore

by general consent ; the considerations involved
being the necessity of rising at ridiculously early
hours, and paying the penalty of sleepy days, to
say nothing of the supremely stupid appearance
which accompanies the countenance of the traveler
who is compelled to turn out in the morning before
he is awake, and swallow his breakfast with an air
ranging between idiocy and despair. So we left
Weldon for Richmond, believing, in the innocence
of our hearts, that it was to Richmond that we were
bound. And such, doubtless, it would have been,
had not the lady in pink happened to lift her eyes
over the top of her magazine as we were rattling
along at a break-neck speed, through forest and
meadow, over hill and vale, and catching a glimpse
of mounting hills and deep green woodland, behind
which a golden sun was setting in a sea of purple,
pass instantaneously from a condition of literary
absorption to a state of bucolic rapture.

"Papa," said she, as she threw open the car-
window for the admission of a simoon of dust and
smoke, "wake up the Pilgrims, please. I have certainly discovered a corner of Paradise. Was there
ever anything one half as beautiful? I wonder if
one could not climb those hills and catch a glimpse
of the Promised Land? Do you imagine they
would stop the train and let us run over there a

half-hour? I shall never be happy unless I do.
Just look at those dear little sheep !" and the goddess fixed her eyes on a bit of plowed ground,
where a score of rooting swine were prospecting
for riches, and went off in a fit of ecstasy.

"Conductor!" shouts the Pharisee, as that worthy chanced to heave in sight, "what is the next
town ?"

"Petersburg, sir."

"Petersburg ? Ah, yes! I remember of knocking
at the door of that inhospitable town in '64, and
being refused admission at the point of the bayo-
net. Is there—a—is there such a thing as a hotel
in—in Petersburg ?"

"Petersburg, sir," responds the conductor, with
mounting wrath, "Petersburg is a city of twenty
thousand people. It has a dozen hotels, street rail-
ways, opera-houses, and—"

"That will do. The opera-houses turn the scale.
We stop at Petersburg."

"But, sir, I have taken up your tickets for Richmond. I really can't change them now, you see."

"Sorry, my dear fellow, if it is going to incon-
venience and embarrass the railroad company, you
know, but the die is cast. We stop at Petersburg,"
and we did. We are diverted from our progress by
the episode of a sunset—thrown off the track by a

drove of pigs! I am afraid there is but a single will among the company. We are no longer free agents ; we are bound hand and foot at the feet of a tyrant in rose-colored lawn.

To be candid, however, I don't know that we regret having tarried a day at Petersburg. It is a town of charming avenues and delightful streets ; of busy workshops and roaring mills and smoking furnaces ; of huge warehouses, where armies of ebony workmen are twisting the narcotic weed in a thousand fanciful shapes, and vast flouring mills, where wheel and burr and fan are converting yellow grain into snowy powder, and trains of drays are loading and unloading barrels and sacks and bags without end. Here the hurrying Appomattox winds in and out, in the midst of luxuriant foliage, dashing here and there, over picturesque falls, and roaring as loudly as though it were Niagara in a rage. Here is a woody hill that conceals a drowsy old cemetery, and Blanford church, severely aristocratic, venerably historic, ivy-mantled and ruined, stands like a grim sentinel, on guard, over miles and miles of grass-grown intrenchments, and dismantled forts, and deserted rifle-pits, and silenced batteries, that tell a story still too painfully vivid for some of us to recall in words.

This morning our party had become inexplicably

scattered. The general and Dora were paying duty-calls among acquaintances in town, Dick with sketch-book and camp-stool had departed to the earth-works, and Jack had engaged a native in a game of billiards, and, as usual in such cases, had happened upon a Tartar; while the Scribe and the Pharisee, left to their own devices, had strolled toward the mounting hills in search of the unconscious swine that had arrested the progress of the pilgrimage.

We had spent an hour in the vicinity of the "Crater," where on that unhappy 30th of July, 1864, so many thousands of brave boys had fallen victims to the dread chance of war, and which, now overgrown with shrubbery and rank grass, laughed with open mouth, as we recalled the hour that—thank God!—lives only in memory. We had strolled over the worn earthworks of Forts Hell and Damnation, where ball and cartridge are still unearthed with easy prod of the cane, and lingered on Cemetery Hill among the graves of thousands, where blue and gray lie together in the sleep that knows no waking, and had smoked the pipe of peace under the walls of the little church at Poplar Spring. Then, spying the old familiar signal-tower which played so prominent a part in the long siege, and was left behind as we hurried away to

Five Forks and victory, we mounted to its very summit, and stretching ourselves at full length, looked off upon a scene of historic beauty.

There lay the busy city gleaming in the sunlight, the smoke of its factories and workshops, the hum of its mills, the roar of the dams and the waterfalls, mingling with the chirping of the birds and the piping of the crickets in the long grass below us. Like a long winding serpent, the glistening Appomattox wound its long length among green fields and golden acres of wheat and nodding corn, hurrying and scurrying to meet the James at City Point. Beyond were mounting hills, dimly lined against the horizon; we seem to see the grove at Appomattox Court House where was ended the wretched tragedy, and the field of Five Forks where it met its Waterloo, and far, far away to the northward, are not those the spires and the smoke of Richmond? And around and about, far, near, and middle-ground, the long lines of hillocks and mounds that tell the story of the long, strong, persistent siege, and the stubborn defense.

Suddenly from our perch we see figures approaching; the hue of pink garments, the long swinging gait of a black-haired Raphael with camp-stool and sketch-book under either arm. They stroll lazily along, laughing, chatting, halt-

ing now and then to admire a bit of landscape—
they pass under the tower and are lost to view.
We wait to see them emerge in the open—but wait
in vain. We peer over the edge at the risk of our
necks. Yes—they are gone. No—we hear them
below under the tower. We cannot dismount—we
care not to interrupt a pleasant conversation—
again we become involuntary listeners.

"Do you know, Miss Dora," says the artist,
"that I am half in love with this sunny land of
yours, with its verdant fields, its languid coast, its
balmy air, its glowing perspective, and its dainty
bits of coloring. Indeed I am wholly in love with
this charming lotos-land. Now there, for instance,
just to the left of us, all unconscious of its beauty,
hangs a perfect Claude. What exquisite tinting!
What noble breadth of landscape! It is a matchless symphony."

"Oh, thank you, Mr. Palette—you flatter us.
By 'us,' you know, I mean myself and my kingdom. I am so proud of my sunny South," and the
goddess draws herself to the full height of her five
feet one, and looks amazingly grateful. There is
measurably more sympathy between Dora and the
artist for manifest reasons. Dick is not a bad-look-
ing fellow for that matter, and to be just to the
scamp, there is really something picturesque and

pleasing about his long waving hair that is black as
the raven's wing, and his fierce, curling moustache
that is bold, brigand-like, and overpowering.   But
bless your heart! there is nothing fierce about Dick.
Dick is the mildest fellow imaginable.   Now there
is Jack, for instance, who affects the haughty and
the severe.   You would never believe it, however,
to look at him.   Who could imagine anything
haughty or severe about a bullet-shaped head from
which the blonde hair has been closely cropped, or
in a pair of liquid blue eyes, or around a hesitating
growth on the upper lip that requires his constant
persuasion to induce to maintain an equilibrium?
As for Sid now—but hold on here!   This is not a
photograph gallery, nor is the Scribe the artist.
On the contrary, that estimable worthy is waiting
to be heard, and we must indulge him.   Dick has
long since discovered a weak point in the armor of
the goddess, and he proposes to make the most of
it.

"Let me congratulate you," says he, "on the incomparable delights of your kingdom.   I could
dream away a lifetime among these leafy composi-
tions, these cool groves, and in this perfect sunlight.

> "'The sunlight of a sunlit land,
>   A land of fruits, of flowers, and

A land of love and calm delight ;
A land where night is not like night,
And noon is but a name for rest ;
Where conversations of the eyes
Are all enough ; where beauty fills
The heart like hues of harvest home ;
Where rage lies down, where passion dies,
Where peace hath her abiding place.' "

"And where, pray, did you discover those perfect lines? Were they written for the South? Has our artist turned poet?"

"Oh, no ; the artist, you know, is always a poet. I believe they are Joaquin Miller's, and Miller is an immense favorite of mine."

"What an absurd taste !" laughs Dora. "What in the world can one fancy about that ridiculous aborigine? He always reminds me of a learned pig."

"I am afraid you are unjust to the aborigine, Miss Dora, for that is principally why I admire him, you see. There is such harmony in his treat-ment, such a *crescendo* in his periods, such *diminu-endo* in his minor chords. His work is made up of the most charming mosaics." Here Sid nearly ex-pired in a fit of strangulation. "But that is not why I admire him the most, Miss Dora. He is a great favorite of mine because he was always in love with a pink countess."

If Dora was not perfectly aware of what was coming, she must have been gifted with less penetration than I have given her credit for. "But all that was pure romance, you know," says she. "The Countess Edna was merely an accessory to the most insipid volume of trash I ever encountered. One cannot be seriously in love with a phantom of one's own creation." How the little sprite can parry the attack! Sid is right; her guard is superb.

"Not in the least," goes on the adversary. "The Countess Edna was a living, breathing reality. She was, and doubtless is, an episode of the Eternal City. She is mated to a neutral-tinted Count whom she selected as a harmonious contrast to her own excessive pinkness; she lives in the most charming and the daintiest of palaces in the street of the Guardian Angel, and she promenades the heights of the Pincio, and loses herself in the ruins of the Coliseum precisely the same as her Roman sisters who are neither rose-colored nor otherwise tinted. In short she was 'the one fair woman.'"

"And was she really a *pink* countess?" How the curiosity of the sex will indulge itself, even in the most trying emergencies!

"She was pink to a fault," says the tempter, "pink, says one who knew her, 'from the roses in

the blonde hair to the tips of the dainty toes ; pink
trimmings on a white gauzy something that only
half obscured an undercurrent of the deepest pink,
that ran all through her. Pink lips, pink ears, and
gloves of the pinkest pink imaginable !' I shall
always love Miller for loving a countess in pink. I
can appreciate his delirium from the madness of
my own. I can—"

" But do you know whether the pink Roman ever
encouraged the aborigine to any extent ?" There's
a thrust for you, Master Dick, that calls for your
most dexterous counter.

"I had rather not continue the narrative," says
he, rather hurriedly. "I admit that the reference
was not altogether happy," and catching a little
smile of triumph on the lips of the goddess, he continued defiantly—what man would not—"You may
re-read the 'One Fair Woman,' Miss Dora, and believe it, word for word. Mind, I don't apologize for
the aborigine—it was a dastardly act at the best—
I merely sympathize with him, you see. He was in
love with a woman in pink."

"Poor aborigine !" comments Dora, in a commis-
erating tone. "How I pity him ! Both for being
in love, and for not preferring a decided color. Now
how much better do we arrange things—we who
are civilized poets—and artists. How culture en-

11·

ables one to discriminate between the real and the
ideal.   You and I, Mr. Palette, would never be
guilty of so absurd a taste, would we ?   Why not ?
I am surprised, Sir Artist, that you should ask such
a question !   Because we know that a tint is only a
suggestion, a hint, an apology for something better."

"But, my dear Miss Dora," says Dick, conscious
that the conversation is wandering from the main
point after all his trouble, "how very inconsistent
you are becoming.   You who are a living example
of the charm of a tint, which to me is the most
adorable of hues.   You see how I argue from cause
to effect."

"How I detest being personal," says the "living
example" with considerable petulance ; "but as you
insist upon compelling me to explain your own
hypotheses, I am driven to the expedient of saying
that you and I are the most unreasonable of beings.
We are creatures of whims and fancies.   It is a
whim of mine to fancy a particular tint in my costume, and a fancy of yours to say that you admire
it.   It is a fancy of mine that you are a most
wretched flatterer, Monsieur Artist, and a whim of
mine to be very much offended.   And now that we
are speaking of whims and fancies, I fancy that the
dinner-hour at the hotel is but fifteen minutes distant, and it is a whim of mine to be nearing the verge

of starvation." And the speakers pass from under the tower and disappear in the grove.

"Poor little goddess!" says Sid, as we descend from our perch and stroll back to town. "Poor little goddess! I wonder if her life is to be made up of this sort of thing. First Jack, now Dick, and I presume it is a mere matter of time before you and I follow suit. Only I'm not exactly in that line, you know, and if I ever catch you at it, my boy, I'll disinherit you. What must she think of us all? There those two wretched scamps, not content with following her about from one end of the land to another, are worrying her life out with their insufferable love-making. I wish I could interfere with any show of reason. If I had only one half the conceit of that shallow-headed Jack, for instance, I would advise her to steal away in the night, without leaving her future address to any of us. We certainly deserve it."

"By the way, Sid," I remark, "have you discovered your octopus yet? The marine creature, you know, whom you encountered in the surf at Old Point. I believe the object of your going to Norfolk was to solve the identity of that mysterious female, and I presume you are making the tour of Virginia on the same delectable errand. Not that I have any concern, you know, for I imagine the whole affair was the result of one of Phœbus's midnight lunches; but, as you seem disposed to attribute ulterior motives to the balance of the party, perhaps you wouldn't mind defining your own."

Sid colors a little before replying, but recovers himself without much emotion beyond an hysterical laugh that induces me to suspect that my feeble little shaft has reached its mark. "I am afraid," said he, "I am afraid, my dear boy, that the mermaid of Old Point will never be discovered, at least not by me. I strongly suspect it to be a dodge of Phœbus's to advertise his house, and induce his victims to linger on as long as their pockets contain a dime. I haven't any manner of doubt that that amphibious female is being regularly carried out to sea every morning, and being as regularly rescued by some sentimental old codger like myself. But, now you have mentioned it, I recall the humiliating fact that I have still about me some doggerel that I was asinine enough to evolve from my aged brain concerning that morning's adventure. I commit it to your tender mercies, my boy. Do what you please with it. It is neither too good for criticism, nor poor enough for ridicule. When you burn it, as you will after reading it, there will disappear the last lingering trace of the mermaid of Old Point."

As we linger over the dessert at the hotel this evening, I am reminded of the lines which had been transferred from Sid's pocket to mine, and as the moment is propitious, I grasp it with no ordinary delight.

"If the company is agreeable," said I, " I desire to call their attention to some thrilling lines that have come into my possession—I shall not say how —and which I am sure your Majesty and the lords in waiting will find of more than ordinary interest. They are—let me see—they are in dactylic measure, and in style of the marine heroic. I observe, by the way, several trifling inaccuracies, which I shall take it upon myself to correct as we proceed. I am always gratified to assist struggling genius. Now, attention company !—eyes right !—listen :

"'A VISION.

"' As I swam in the breakers one morning,
    Tossed about by a swift, heavy sea,
Carelessly, recklessly drifting,
    A vision there came to me.
I seemed to see floating beyond me
    One, fair as the morning was bright ;
One, drifting about in the breakers,
    Sinking within my sight.
    (*Sight, sight. A-sinking within my sight.*) '

"I hope it is needless for me to remark that the refrain is my own amendment. I am not sure but I could have thrown together something better upon mature reflection; but no well-considered poem is complete without a chorus or a refrain, or something of that sort, you know. Attention company!—no levity in the ranks, if you please—this is not a minstrel show!—listen to the *antistrophe :*

> "'It was all a dream, but I hastened
>   To rescue that perishing one.
>   (*That must have been a lively old dream.*)
>   One effort, one struggle, 'twas done.
>   And yet, as I felt her clasping arms,
>   And her heart to mine so near,
>   I thought that no vision was half so sweet.
>   (*I should rather say not, my dear,*
>   *Dear, dear! No vision was half so queer.*)'"

"What the mischief was it all about, any way?" says Jack. "Did he have the nightmare? Do the verses give any clue to the perpetrator of the outrage?"

"Well, no, Jack; but this is certainly an example of the very *delirium tremens* of poetry. Let me give you an improved version of another stanza.

> "'For now each morning and evening
>   That vision returns to me
>   (*Till I've got a bad case of rheumatics*
>   *From bathing in the cold, cold sea*).

But never again shall I hold her,
Of all womankind, the pearl.
(*But I'll wager at the present moment*
He's holding some other girl,
Girl, girl. He is spooning to some other girl.)'

"But I trust the pilgrims will comprehend the situation. The cold morning—the tumbling breakers—the despairing cry—the rescue, and the other girl in the distance. It is a glowing panorama, a—"

"Now, Mr. Wright!" interrupts Dora, "I shall not be a party to such wretched wrangling of those splendid lines. Give them to me, please. I have a fancy for seeing what they are all about." I wonder if that was a blush I detected on the cheeks of the goddess, or merely a reflection from the pinky pinkness of her costume.

"Saul, my boy," says the Pharisee, "your precocity will certainly hasten your demise. Give the lines to Miss Dora, or better still, throw them in the fire. Who cares to peep into somebody's secret?"

"Miss Dora shall have the lines—after the company have listened to the epode. And out of regard for your feelings, my dear Pharisee, I will let you have them *verbatim.*"

"You shall do nothing of the kind," and the

blush becomes an angry frown. "Give me the paper as it is, or not at all." And I meekly obey, feeling that we have all been cheated out of our revenge. Why should the goddess have cared for those silly lines? And why should the Pharisee wear such a confusing expression, as she hides them in her bosom, and peers over at him from under her long eyelashes?

Perplexedly,

SAUL WRIGHT.

X.

SPECTRAL ANALYSIS.

RICHMOND, VA.,
September 15, 18—.

THE first softening shades of an autumn twilight
are closing in around the pathway where a red sun
has sunk to rest behind purple curtains, as we stand
on the crest of Libby Hill, and watch the cool gray
waters of the James, as they flow silently by the
side of glowing verdure, and in long sweeping arcs
wind proudly around low-lying hills, on their way
to the welcoming, ever-exacting sea. Behind us,
like a long matchless avenue, whose outlet is lost
in the growing shadows, stretches the Main street
of Richmond, down which we follow with fixed
eye, and seem to feel the throbbing pulse of the
busy city, as it weakens and wanes toward the close
of the day's toil. It is the one happy point from
which one can see all there is to see of Richmond.
Over against the horizon are the heights of Holly-
wood, the apex of whose pyramidal pile, sacred to
the memory of the dead who died in vain, pierces
the purple clouds, and far away to the westward

are the groves of Oakwood, where eighteen thousand marble slabs rise over the mounds where
sleep an army of the " Boys in Gray." Before us
lies the city, where dull red chimneys vie to soar
with piercing church-spires, and huge white flouring mills and low black foundries contest the
field with iron warehouses and elegant abodes, and
in their midst uprises the severe white porticoes of
a new Parthenon. In one bold sweeping vista we
embrace the patient river and the impetuous town,
the heights and the gardens, the parks, the bridges,
the green fields, and the narrow lanes. And the
coming twilight settles down and enwraps the picture as in a mantle.

The general is the first to break the silence.
"We are standing," said he, "where once stood the
royal wigwam of the mighty Powhatan. As nearly
as may be on this very spot, this great chieftain of
all the tribes between the James and the Rappahannock, and from the falls to the sea, abode in
barbaric splendor. His body-guard of forty chosen
warriors surrounded him by day, and by night four
huge sentinels kept watch and ward about his
royal person. His domain was an empire, and his
brave subjects roamed these broad fields, and made
these mighty forests ring with their merry voices,
or resound with their shrill battle cries. It was the

land of Powhatan. The broad river that flows beneath us was the Powhatan ; the confederation of the twenty tribes was the Powhatan—in the sense that we say Germany, when we mean the German confederation—and the supreme ruler of all was the Pharaoh, the Kaiser, the King, the Emperor, the sublime and incomparable Brother of the Sun, the mighty Powhatan. I presume, with all reasonable accuracy, we may say that we stand in the footsteps of royalty."

"And with historical accuracy, general," says the Scribe, "permit me to add, now that you have located the spot, where, about this time of the year, a trifle of two hundred and seventy-two years ago, came one Smith, a pilgrim like ourselves, a Smith with the humble prefix of John, and in the presence of the sublime and incomparable Brother of the Sun—and standing at the very foot of the throne itself—proceeded to divest royalty of its possessions, as coolly as the nation he represented has appropriated to itself almost everything that has come in its way ever since. 'Let me see,' said he, 'what did I hear your Majesty call this river below us ? The Powhatan ? I don't like it ! Your Majesty, permit me to remark, has a most vulgar taste. Suppose we call it the *James*. That sounds better ; and, besides, it will remind you of a distinguished gentleman who is a particular friend of mine in England. And your country I believe you also call Powhatan. What a strange liking you appear to have for that jaw-breaking word. Now don't you think *Virginia* would sound better? There's a lady on the other side whom we were in the habit of flattering by calling the Virgin Queen. And while I am about it, I trust your sublime Majesty will pardon me, for taking formal possession of your dominion in the name of King James of England. It is merely a little custom of ours, you know. Good morning.'"

"Ah, yes," said Sid; "that was the beginning of our Indian policy. Go on, general, please; the Scribe's remarks are in parenthesis."

"I hope the Scribe will permit us the enjoyment of our little romance," says the general with a smile. "We haven't enough in this country to hurt. Well, Powhatan had a brother who rejoiced in the delightful name of Opechancanough, and who was king of Pamunkey. This brave old fellow happened to be standing about at the time the gentleman by the name of Smith was taking such liberties with his brother's possessions, and in his ignorance failed to see the point of the joke which the Smith party aforesaid doubtless designed to perpetrate. So he laid in wait for him on his next visit to Richmond, captured him without much trouble, and tying him hand and foot, brought him to the presence of our friend, the Brother of the Sun, who was spending the summer at Werowoco-moco, which I presume was a watering-place on the York River. Here he was tried by a jury of his peers and sentenced to death. His head was laid on the cold, cold stone, the executioners had lifted their huge weapons of death, when a loud cry was heard, and the lovely daughter of the king, the fair Poca—"

" Now, see here, general," interrupts Jack, "what are you giving us ? Hasn't that Pocahontas story been exploded long ago ?"

" It has, Jack," says the Scribe. " It has, alas ! it has. But go on, general, if you please; the Scribe's remarks are in parenthesis."

" I am afraid," says the man of war, " I am afraid there is a painful absence, among the pilgrims, of that sympathy and imagination which should ac-company all well-regulated romances. I abdicate the throne of the late Powhatan, who I don't im-agine was much of an emperor after all."

And so we throw ourselves on the grassy knoll as the dim twilight settles down upon the river, and the groves and the hills are hid in the blue, vapory mists of evening. Now from the city bright lights are peeping out from amid the trees ; the long, narrow avenue becomes a glittering lane, where two parallel lines of twinkling stars are crossed here and there by diagonal and transverse columns that form fanciful figures of glowing sparks ; the foundries emit huge flames, and, serpent-like, a long train of lighted cars winds out from amid the lighted houses and rumbles across a lighted bridge. The chirp of insect life, but a moment since so busy around us, the hum of minute existence, the chatter of birds, is hushed ; nature has entered upon her season of rest. Then, one by one, the bright silver stars come peeping forth, like little twinkling sparks in space, till the heavens are studded with their myriads ; the Milky Way, like a broad rainbow, stretches across the heavens, and Ursa Major stands out like a diamond ornament on the bosom of beauty. And as we watch, up comes the full, round moon, attended by a group of fleecy clouds, and soars into a field already overflowing with radiant gems.

"How delightful is the night," says the general again, between the pauses of a rambling conversation wherein the goddess had been pleased to make merry over the imaginary joys and sorrows of the fair daughter of sturdy Powhatan. "I am reminded, as I lounge here on Libby Hill, of another night

in the long ago, quite as fair and lovely and delightful as this. You have been pleased, my boys,
to suppress my attempts to render the scene roman-
tic. Do you care to listen to the o'er-true tale of
an old soldier who struggled through two long, terrible campaigns in and around this fated city, and
struggled, alas! in vain?" And we are all attention
as the veteran of a "lost cause" throws from him
the remains of his cigar, and braces himself against
the trunk of a towering chestnut.

"It was evening of one of those terrible days in
the Wilderness," said he, in an unsteady voice
which induced us to suspect something unusual in
the coming story, and to gather about him in re-
spectful silence. "The fight had been raging hot
all day along the whole line, and the slaughter had
been merciless, terrible, murderous. Four times
had my brigade been driven from its position, four
times had we rallied and swept the enemy from the
disputed ground; but each time with diminished
ranks, each effort costing us dearly, as we left behind one after another of the brave fellows who
were glad to die that their fair land might live; and
each time as we regained the ground it was to find
it a fresh slaughter-house of the dead, the mangled,
and the dying. At last Grant in person had discovered the tenacity with which we held the knoll,

and hurling fresh thousands upon us, had driven our worn, bleeding columns to the woods, and pressing his advantage, hunted us man by man, from tree and bush and sheltering rock, capturing, killing, maiming, until that once grand, unrivaled brigade, that the brave boys had been pleased to greet as 'Fisher's Legion,' existed only in memory.

"Some kind, protecting influence had unaccountably hovered about me through that terrible day. I had passed unscathed the brunt of the fight, and perhaps in my blasphemous conceit had believed my poor frame impenetrable and sacred, when in that last fearful onslaught a minie ball entered my chest; my horse—poor, faithful friend! —had been shot from under me, crushing my leg in his fall; a saber cut had laid open my cheek. Then in his last dying struggles I saw the iron hoof of my dumb companion descending on my head—a ringing, stunning blow—a sudden blinding numbness—ten thousand fiery fantastic sparks passed before my eyes, and I knew no more.

"How long I had lain on the field I knew not. I awoke to feel a heavy, crushing weight on my lower limbs; to see a clear, starry dome above me, through which a round, mellow moon was slowly climbing; to hear about me groans and moans, with now and then a piercing shriek, or the whin-

nying of horses. Then came a quieting numbness. I wondered why I was there ; why the moon
traveled so slowly and the stars shone so brightly ;
why I could not rise ; why I should care to ; why I
had ever cared to lie elsewhere than on the soft
bosom of mother earth, and with heaven's blue,
studded vault above me. Then came a sensation
of pain ; of an inability to move hand or foot ; of a
choking, maddening thirst. A wrenching attempt
to relieve my leg from its crushing load brought
on me a sharp, quick pain ; my brain began to
throb lazily, hotly, and now to burn with liquid
fire and shooting, devilish pains. And the terrible,
choking thirst—the agony—the torments of the
damned swept through me with every breath, and
the coursing of the hot blood through my burning
veins. 'O my God!' I cried, 'hasten in pity to
deliver me from this horrible bondage !' and I
shrieked aloud in my agony.

"Then I heard a voice near me, the voice of
another sufferer who I found was lying not far
away from my grassy couch. 'Be patient!' said
the voice. 'I am coming as soon as I can lift this
confounded dead man from my chest'—then a
pause, and a straining from the voice. Then I
heard it again. 'What a cussed assurance a man
must have to lie down and die on another man's

breast!' it says. Now a tall, slim figure looms up
in the moonlight like a specter. It strides toward
me—it bends over me—a ghastly, horrid countenance, from which the blood was dripping from an
open wound across the ghastly cheek!—burning
eyeballs glared out from amidst a tangled beard!
'Great God, man!' it said, 'how can you bear the
weight of this monstrous beast and live? And I
think you have a gray uniform. What a wretched
taste! And your head is as icy and cold as a woman's
heart! Well, my old friend and enemy, you have
fought your last fight, so I don't know that there
is any objection to my rendering aid and comfort—
is there?' Then I felt my limbs released, as the
terrible load was being slowly pried away, and
again the tall, bloody specter leaned over me, and I
felt its hot breath on my cheeks and its fiery eyes
peering into mine.

"'Now, my friend,' said the voice, 'if you will
take my advice you will let me bury you quietly
under the daisies. Life is so little worth living
at the best, and to you I really think this is an
opportunity that should not be neglected. To-
morrow morning some one will come along and
throw you into a trench with all sorts of miscel-
laneous rabble, and cover you over with a layer of
quick-lime, and that will be the last of you. I am

not sure that I could carve out much of a grave for you, old fellow, but I would do my best, and it would certainly be preferable to going through the balance of life without arms or legs. You don't think so? What execrable taste! By Jove! I've a mind to leave you to your own devices. Or shall I bury you while I have the strength? I don't know how long it will last, you know. What! you are thirsty? Drink? water? Why, man, that might prolong your life! Well, your blood be upon your own head. I'll do my best, but upon my word, you'll never forgive me if I should happen to save your life.'

"Then I felt the mouth of a flask pressed to my burning lips—a gurgling, a bubbling, and streams of liquid life were pouring down my parched throat, and coursing through my stiffened veins. Then I felt arms about me—a sensation of being lifted as gently as a child in the arms of this cheerful specter, and being borne slowly, staggeringly along over the black corpses and amid the ranks of groaning humanity. Once or twice we stumbled and fell—the strength of my specter was evidently failing—and I remember of wondering whether he was not as feeble as myself, of wishing I had the power to resist his humane endeavors, and of wondering whether he hadn't better have buried me decently after all. Then as my head hung listlessly over his arm, the full moon came out from a shadow, and lightened up the figure of a silver eagle on a yellow ground, as it gleamed and glittered on his shoulder. But once he spoke, and then to ask where I would be taken. I could merely whisper my name and rank, and the name of General Lee, and I remember next the challenge of our pickets—that I was being lifted from his arms to a stretcher, and then of being borne along in comfort with the tall specter beside me, a prisoner of war. Then, as speech was denied me, I pulled an onyx ring from my finger—an old heirloom on which was engraved a lion *couchant*—pressed it into the hand of my specter, and I remember no more.

"A month later, as I arose from a long siege of brain fever, my first inquiry was for my specter of the Wilderness. 'He has gone to Salisbury,' said the grizzly old sergeant who had attended me, 'and I reckon from there to Andersonville. He was a Yankee colonel, you know, who refused to give his name, and when we were going to send him to Libby with the other officers, he tore his eagles from his shoulders, and demanded to be treated like the rest of the boys of his regiment. Begging your pardon, general, he was the d—dest fool I ever

heard of! To think of a man going to Andersonville when he might have gone to Libby! So long
as he wore his straps, you know, he was a "parole-
of-honor-man," and then he called at the hospital
every morning and evening to hear how you were
getting along, and it was a queer coincidence,
wasn't it, sir, that it was the morning you were pro-
nounced out of danger when he ripped off his eagles
and fell in line with the squad for Salisbury.'

"'But,' I persisted, 'did no one recognize him
among our men? Did no one know his name and
regiment?'

"'Oh, yes, sir!' said the sergeant with a grin;
'we knew him to be the biggest and most reckless
dare-devil in the Yankee army, and he's killed
enough of our boys to be drawn and quartered.
But we didn't know his name—oh, no, sir—only that
he was a cavalry colonel and a dangerous enemy.
It was a grand prize you brought in that night,
general. Who would have thought of so queer a
dodge but you? To think of bringing in a big prisoner, all cut and bleeding as you were! Why, the
whole camp has been laughing over it ever since.'

"'But, great Scott, man!' I gasped, 'I didn't
bring him in. It was he who brought *me* in. It
was the bravest, most generous act of the whole
war. He ran his head into the lion's mouth to

save me. Do you hear? To save me! To save the life of your old general, who, but for him, would now be lying underneath the sod of the Wilderness! Hurry, sergeant,' I shouted, 'hurry to General Lee, and with my compliments, say I demand the immediate release of the bravest man that ever lived. Do you hear me? Go!' and exhausted with the effort I fell over in a faint, and a relapse sent me under the blankets for another month.

"But bless your hearts, it was of no use. General Lee was kindness itself, and we searched every prison in the South, but no one knew of his fate. Here and there, some one would remember a tall, fair man with an ugly saber cut across his face, first at Danville, then at Salisbury, at Florence, and then we traced him among the thousands of poor wretches at Andersonville, whose numbers were so vast and our means so limited that they lived and died and were thrown into the trenches and forgotten. I have always lived in the hope that some day I should find him, that some time in the future—maybe beyond the grave—I should place my hand in his, and tell him that the old rebel general has not forgotten. If he be dead, I mourn him always. If living, were he to demand the half my kingdom, I would deem the price too poor and mean for his acceptance. For, gentlemen, but for him I should never have been blessed, in the winter of my age, with the dear, precious love and companionship of my little Dora. God knows what she has been to me! Wife, sons, home, friends, all have departed, and I have none but her to cherish, and to cheer my declining years."

Then with a glad little cry our goddess threw herself into the arms of the grim old soldier, and I am afraid she was not the only one of the pilgrims whose eyes watered with tears that were irresistible and uncontrollable. "Wasn't that a brave deed?" said she, through her tears. "I have heard it a hundred times, and I always cry over it as though it were all new and sudden to me, don't I, papa? It seems to me that the man who could do that was greater than a king. Don't you think so, Mr. Pharisee?"

"Well, I don't see anything so very brave in it," says that worthy, true and constant to his name, as he lighted a cigarette. "It was only his duty, you know. War is a terrible affair at the best, you see, and when a man takes his life in his hands, it don't matter much how he throws it away. And then you see the general happens to be an interested party, which, besides making him a partial narrator, imbues the little episode with an interest that concerns us all, because the general is our friend, and a most excellent story-teller. Now, for instance, were the late Captain John Smith among us this evening, to repeat that little scene with Pocahontas and the cold, cold stone, we should all doubtless have pictured the affair as among the most delightful adventures of history. Miss Dora, please do not look at me in that way! I mean no offense to the specter of the Wilderness, you know, who I have no doubt was an excellent fellow in his way, and possibly enjoyed the affair quite as much as the general."

"But think of his taking papa right into our camp, when he might have taken him to his own and made *him* a prisoner."

"I have thought of everything, Miss Dora. There was no good of his taking a dying man to his enemies, you know. If I remember correctly, we had about as many of our own men on our hands about that time as we could take care of, and he was probably too good a Yankee to put his government to the expense of burying a rebel general. I have thought of everything, and among the myriad of my thoughts on this moonlit occasion, I am thinking that the dews are falling, the grass is becoming damp, and the general's doleful story has sent a cold chill down my back, and unless I am mistaken,

I have noticed your ladyship shivering within the last moment. Suppose we return to town."

And so, as the full yellow moon is climbing slowly into the starry blue, and the hills, parks, gardens, and the river are taking on a mellow hue; as the chill dews are descending, and a light vapory fog rising from the low lands and surrounding the city, through which the gaslights are twinkling and blinking ; and as the low, silvery bells are ringing the hour when the good people of Richmond are expected to put out their lights and jump into bed, we stroll back to town.

Sleepily,

SAUL WRIGHT.

XI.

OFT IN THE STILLY NIGHT.

HYGEIA HOTEL, OLD POINT COMFORT, VA.,
September 28, 18—.

OUR Richmond visit, which had not contemplated the stay of beyond a day or so, has lengthened by the most delightful of processes to a fortnight. There were calls to be made and returned,
boating parties on the sweeping James, and carriage rides along the hard, shady country roads,
horseback parties along the Williamsburg pike and
the gravely road that sweeps along the Kanawha.
There was a quiet little excursion to the Luray
Caves, and a picnic to a strange little grove on the
Totopotomoi. How the labors of the Scribe would
be interminably lengthened should he attempt to
elaborate from the mere suggestions of his note-
book ! Then there were mornings in the tobacco
factories, where we listened to expositions of bewildering industry, and watched the nimble fingers
of dusky minstrels as they twisted and turned the
brown, shining leaf into plugs and cables and
twists, to the accompaniment of ballads, whereof

the sorrows of the late Daniel Tucker and a female by the name of Susanna were pathetically portrayed. There were hours in the flouring mills, and a midnight experience at the Tredegar Iron Works, where, amid molten iron and liquid brooks of fire, and gaunt moving specters and demons, darting here and there amid the flames, we were enabled to account for the skepticism of Bobingersol, regarding the character of a future state. It was a fortnight that leaves an impression of enjoyable comfort, a confused idea of crowding into a single experience the superlatives of laziness and industry ; a fortnight in which the whole resources of the State of Virginia, including atmosphere and vegetation, were concentrated about the pathway of a few strolling pilgrims.

In the order of their occurrence, let me, instead of becoming a paltry narrator of sights and sounds, endeavor to give you the record of some startling events in the lives of the pilgrims. You see I have not entirely recovered from the shock of precipitated surprises which have descended upon me within the past week, and am hardly expected to be altogether coherent. To begin with, I was not at all satisfied with the manner with which Sid had contrived to monopolize the company of our sole and solitary maiden during the stay at Richmond.

Sid has been my particular companion, you know, during the most of the pilgrimage. I was vexed to find myself wholly deserted. I was no little displeased to find that my occasional walks and talks with her ladyship herself were no longer possible, owing to the aforesaid monopolization and the desertion aforementioned. It began to look very much, you see, like cause and effect. Whenever I attempted to hunt up my Inseparable for a game of billiards, or an after-dinner stroll with a cigar accompaniment, it was to hunt for an hour in vain, and then to discover him in cosy *tête-à-tête* with Miss Dora, and looking precisely as though he would look upon an interruption as a deadly insult. Were I to stumble upon an excellent paragraph in the morning paper, or an exquisite bar of music at the piano, which I knew that Dora would thoroughly appreciate, I was absolutely certain to find her discussing some abstruse point in small-talk with Sid, so totally at variance with the character of my own discovery, that I knew my interference would constitute the unpardonable sin. I ran against them at all hours and in the most unexpected places. I stumbled upon them at the strangest out-of-the-way nooks, and happened upon them at the most embarrassing moments. Jack and Dick I didn't particularly affect, and the general was persistently engaged with his old friends and companions-in-arms about town. So you see the thing at last became unendurable, and not to be longer tolerated.

The bubble of my swollen indignation burst one evening as Sid and myself sat alone in our room at the Exchange just before retiring.

" Sid, old fellow," said I, " I've a big bone to pick with you, and the sooner it's off my mind the better. I am not going to reproach you for your sudden desertion, you know; for, being an American citizen, vested with the pursuit of life, liberty, and happiness, in your own vulgar manner, you have a right to your own associates, which the long intimacy of years has no right to affect. But what I particularly object to is being deserted for a woman—a woman in pink—and from the First Families—who delights in pink, you know, for the reason that she would be hideous in any other color, and a perfect fright in white, etc., etc."

"Now Saul, my boy," says the Pharisee, after permitting me to conclude in my most scathing inflection, "I beg of you—don't try that style ! It don't become you, and besides it's awfully vulgar. I presume I once used some language that sounded something like that, but did it ever occur to you that were it not for exceptions there would be no such thing as rules ? And besides that was before

I knew Do—Miss Fisher.   I am prepared to apologize, you know, as regards that sweeping abstract."

"But, Sid, that isn't all of it.   I am not thinking
so much of you as of her.   Knowing your own
feelings so well, you see, I cannot see why in the
world you care to make a fool of that dear little
thing who has never injured you, and to whom we
are all indebted for so many, many kindnesses.
Why need you so monopolize her society ?   Why
need you fill her head so full of your own cynical
ideas, besides teaching her to become interested in a
fellow that is only carrying on a wretched flirtation
at the best ?   You know, old fellow, as well as I do,
that it can end in nothing that you will have any
right to be proud of, and may result in something
you will be ashamed of.   Sid, you and I have been
long and intimate companions—need I say, friends ?
I expect I care more for your friendship than for
that of any other man living ; but, sooner than see
you imbitter the future of Dora Fisher, I will go to
the general and out with the whole story.   Now,
my dear Sid, you may put that in your pipe and
smoke it."

"I don't think, old fellow, you need go as far as
that, for I can save you the trouble.   You are right
and you are wrong.   Right in saying that it must
come to an end, and wrong in the thought that I

would harm one hair of her dear little head. Yes, it must end, as you say, and the sooner the better," and Sid stares straight ahead of him, and puffs away at his pipe gloomily and despairingly.

"Of course I knew you would see it as I do," I respond, penitent and mollified in a moment, for really Sid is a fellow that I am proud of. "I was positive that an appeal to your own good judgment would not be in vain. But, Sid, old chap, now that is settled, be candid, won't you, for once in your life ? Don't you think you are touched just a trifle ? Do you think that every man is a confounded maniac who happens to be in love—with a woman ? Haven't you 'any patience with a man in love'? Sid, if I'm any judge from appearances, your wings are certainly scorched a trifle this time. Isn't it the old story of the moth and the candle ? And, by Jove, I don't blame you ! She's the dearest little woman in all the world, and it was an unfortunate moment for her when she took the whim into her dear little head to be kind and gracious to such a set of wretched Bohemians as we. Be honest for once, Sid, confess like a man, and I'll promise to let you off, and never breathe the matter again."

Judge then of my surprise when Sid buries his face in his hands on the table, and trembles all over

with the agonies of suppressed emotion. "He has
it bad—poor old fellow !" I say to myself. Why
the mischief will a fellow run his head into danger
with his eyes wide open ? I leave him with his
trouble, and filling my pipe, stroll out into the hall.
Just as I close our own door, I notice the door of
the room adjoining close softly, but not too quickly
for me to detect the pale, troubled face of our dear
little goddess almost hid in the wealth of the dead
golden hair that fell about her white-robed shoulders. Great heavens ! thought I, why had I not
known that between her room and ours was nothing but the thinnest and scantiest apology for a
partition ? I hasten back to warn Sid of the fact,
cursing myself for my folly, and heaping impreca-
tions on the heads of the wretches who have managed to accomplish precisely the mischicf that they
wished to avoid. As I entered, Sid sprang to his
feet, pale, haggard, and tearful, and before I could
restrain him, burst into a torrent of words.

"My dear old fellow," said he, as he grasped my
shoulders with either hand, "you have guessed my
wretched secret. Our sweet little goddess is dearer
to me than all the world. I have struggled to
avoid it, my boy, but it is useless. I find that she
fills every part of my being, that sleeping or waking I can think of nothing but her, and that I would

count the world well lost to gain one little atom of her great, honest love. I love her, old chum!— Great God, how I love her! I scarcely knew how much myself until I see the whole wretched, useless folly of it. But thank Heaven, she will never know it! That much is within my power, old fellow. I can strangle it, you know, and she need be no whit the wiser. Oh, if it could only be! What madness *that* is! What have I to give her in return for her dear, sweet, precious self? To think of a poor devil of a fellow like me presuming to love her at all, and then of thinking she could by any manner of means return it. What a stupid and egregious fool I have made of myself. Had I the least thought that she has suspected this madness of mine I should be inclined to beat out my brains in despair. No, don't fear, old fellow, she knows nothing, and please God, she never shall! I can save her that much, you know."

Then grasping his hat he flung open the door and rushed down the passage before I could restrain him, or whisper one word of my discovery. In fact, I am not sure but I had forgotten it altogether in witnessing this unsuspected trouble of my dear old Inseparable. Where in the world can he be going, I wonder? May he not be projecting some terrible method of crushing out this hopeless

13

passion? But pshaw! that's all nonsense. Sid is
too much of a man to be anything at all of a boy.
He has a natural desire to be alone with his trouble,
and would look upon my following him an imper-
tinence, I think. But I prepared to follow him,
nevertheless. As I close my door to pass down the
hall, I am confronted by the great, round, frightened
eyes and the pale face of Dora. She has thrown on
the pinkest of pink wrappers, and has twisted the
loose locks into the veriest attempt in the world at
anything like order, and is cold, wan, disheveled,
trembling, and a thousand times more charming
than ever.

"Go after him!" she whispers, in the tearful
voice that has always charmed us into sympathy
whenever we have encountered it during the changes
of the pilgrimage. "Go quick, and overtake him,
and tell him that Dora expects him in the parlor at
once! Don't take 'no' for an answer, and bring
him back if you care for me. Don't wait an instant,
please, *please* don't, or you compel me to follow him
myself."

And so I hurry out into the night. A dark,
gloomy night, in which the darkness is painful as
I emerge from the hotel and feel my way through
the long side passage that leads to the street where
the dim gaslights are trying to burn, and dim shad-

ows are chasing each other in and out of the trees
of the park. How useless, I think, as I gaze up
and down the deserted street, and peer into the
gloomy park, scarce lighted by the few straggling
beams from the few straggling lanterns, and stride
hopelessly along the brick pavements that echo my
footsteps against the granite walls. How hopeless,
I think, to chase a man who is seeking solitude,
through the streets of a dark city, where nothing
but shadows and dreariness and gloom and mist
are abroad. What a bootless, foolish errand I am
on! What an absurd, fruitless, hopeless chase!
What a preposterous dunderhead I was to have
attempted it! Then I think of the pale, patient
little goddess waiting alone in the parlor—waiting
for some one that never may come; waiting in confidence and trust in my ability to bring him back;
waiting for Heaven knows what in the end, and I
hurry along. Up this street and down that—through
park and garden where we have lounged and loafed
—here, there, everywhere, but where I know not.
And the dull clanging bell rings out the hour
of midnight ; a low whistle sounds from some be-
lated train outside the city; some gloomy night-
owl hoots from the depths of a huge, somber
wood. Then I climb slowly up the crest of Shockoe
Hill, and turning into Capitol Square, sink down on

a rustic bench, where a spectral fountain is trick-
ling and dripping in the gloom, and try to think it
all over.

It is all my fault, I ponder to the fountain. No
one's but mine. Why could I not have left "well
enough" alone? Why need I to have interfered in
the wretched affair? What business was it of
mine, anyhow? Could I not have trusted in Sid's
honor, and in her own honest heart, that deemed
no guile when none was intended and none possible? What a wretched mess I have managed to
make of it all! It was well enough as it was; why
could I not have left it alone? But *was* it well
enough? Was it well to have had the useless, listless, purposeless intimacy go on? Has not Sid himself admitted the folly of it? Has he not confessed
that my thoughtless interference has awakened him
to the truth? Has he not said what was terribly,
pitilessly true, that he had nothing to give her in return for her love? Yes, it is best as it is. Better
to have had the awakening than the fear of it.
Better to have loved and lost, than never— And
then comes the thought of that solitary little
maiden alone in the cheerless parlor, waiting—for
what? For me—for some one that I was to bring
—for one that I know no more the hiding of than
she herself. Oh, what a wretched, miserable, des-

olate, heart-broken, accursed end of our pilgrimage !

Then a tall, gloomy, specter-like form emerges
from the shadows, and confronts me.

" For God's sake, old fellow !" it says, "what can
you be doing here? Why did you not await my
return ? I have been walking it off, you know—
trying to get rid of the whole wretched load—and
it is all right now. And you shall not blame yourself, dear old chap, for anything. You were right
and I was wrong. It all came from my accursed
presumption, you know—from the conceited idea
that I could play with my own heart. It is all for
the best, and you knew it so much better than I.
Don't you worry, my dear old boy, about her.
Bless your heart, she hasn't an idea of it ! Don't
you know she never has given me so much as a single iota of encouragement—not so much as a whisper—a sign—a suspicion ? It has been all my own
accursed conceit. I have merely singed my own
wings, don't you see, in hovering around a pink
candle. See—a pink candle ! Ha ! ha ! the joke is
on me, you know, this time. By Jove, how Jack
would enjoy it all ! I've a mind to punish myself
by telling him the whole ridiculous story. Come—
let us go home. What a wretched, dark, gloomy
night it is, by the way. Saul, my boy, I really be-

lieve you are feeling as badly as I was over it all. As I *was*, you hear, for you see I have strangled it now, and I defy the fates to resurrect it."

"Oh, yes," think I, as we pace slowly back to the hotel, arm in arm, Sid as jolly and merry as a mountebank, pitiably, hysterically merry, "oh, yes; maybe you have strangled it, my boy; maybe it is all a joke that Jack would enjoy; maybe you have only singed your wings with a pink candle, and all that sort of thing; but, my dear old mountebank, you don't know that that same dear little pink candle is burning brightly in the parlor at the hotel, and unless I am very much mistaken, your wings are going to be clipped clean to your shoulders before you are through with it. It is possible that you may have walked it off; but if you only knew it, my boy, you are walking it on again, with every step you are taking toward home." So we reach the hotel, and the loud bells clang out one o'clock as we turn down the dark passage, and the night clerk sleepily opens one eye long enough to wonder if we are both sober, and I lead the way along the corridor, and halt at the door of the parlor. "I have an odd fancy to look in here a moment," I exclaim, and Sid obediently, wonderingly follows. A light is dimly burning in the low chandelier, the chairs, the lounges, and the piano stand out in the shadows, and the deep rich hue of the carpets and the heavy window hangings shed a warm glow over the scene. Then a graceful little pink figure starts up from a *fauteuil* by the window, and I prepare to withdraw. "Stay!" says the goddess, and I obey.

Why? Not to listen, mind you. Bless your heart, didn't I know the whole familiar story from the moment I departed in search of the wanderer? Didn't I know what was to be said, and how the whole splendid truth was to come out at the end? Oh, no, not to listen—I stayed for a nobler purpose. I had been driven into this unfortunate *rôle* of a confidant, and my duty was not ended. I had played at my own instigation the part of a cautioning friend to Sid; at his, I had become a father confessor; at hers, a courier. And now, by the general, intuitive consent of all parties, I wind up in the character of Monsieur Propriety. But bless your hearts again, neither of them remembered I was there after the first moment. I might as well have been at the massacre at Cabul for all they knew. But let it be distinctly understood, should it ever come out, that the secret of our little goddess was told in a dimly-lighted public parlor in a hotel in Richmond at one o'clock in the morning, that I was there, and heard it.

"Sid," said she, as she threw herself into the wondering arms of the lucky scamp, "you dear old Sid, do you know that I heard every word of your conversation with Saul in your room to-night? Do you know that I know that you love me? Don't you know that your room is next to mine, and that I listened at the partition, for fear I should lose a single word? Don't you know, my poor old darling, that I am the happiest girl in all the world? O my love! I could not wait until morning, for fear you might slip away from me," and here the tearful voice was lost in the flow from the tearful eyes.

"Can it be true, Dora?" he inquires, in a tone that is choking and hollow. "Can it be that you, too, are going to be miserable over this unfortunate, unhappy passion? How much better, my darling, that we never had met. Do I love you? Great God, I love your very shadow, my darling. But what is the good of it? Of me, poor, homeless, friendless, miserable, to claim the love that is dearer to me than life. I cannot ask you to marry me, my precious. I dare not! God help us both, I dare not!"

"Then, you dear old Pariah—if you will have it so—if you are not going to ask me, then you put me to the trouble of asking you. Don't you remem-

ber that I once said that whenever I wanted anything very, very much, I would not be ashamed to
ask for it ?" ·

"Do I remember? Don't I remember every little foolish speech you have ever made through these
six long weeks?"

"Then, Sir Pharisee," says the goddess, sinking
in mock humility on one knee, "will you permit
me to tender you my heart and hand, and beg on
bended knee that you deign in your graciousness
to accept the trifling gift I have the honor to tender?"

Then, stooping, he lifted her bodily in his long,
strong arms and gathered her closely to his heart.
Then, as we all sat cosily together on the huge
sofa by the window, and exchanged remembrances,
and concocted plans, and built the most elaborate of castles, there occurred incidents and episodes
and digressions that it would not become a mere
Scribe to divulge. You would enjoy the narrative
—oh, I am sure you would—but wild horses shall
never tear those details from my breast.

Obstinately,

SAUL WRIGHT.

XII.

WE left Richmond one morning on the saucy little steamer *Ariel* to return to Old Point. For many reasons we had decided that the pilgrimage should end at the point of departure. There were associations surrounding that watery retreat that to two foolish pilgrims, at least, demanded a revisit if not a renewal of experiences. It was, furthermore, another stage on the route of our return to the busy world of the Scribe and the Pharisee, and not altogether out of the way for the poet and the artist. Then the general had insisted upon tendering the pilgrims a farewell dinner, and what banqueting-hall could be more appropriate, or what caterer more entitled to the honor of serving it, than the delightful Hygeia, and its jolly old Boniface? And then besides all this, I am positive that there was not a single member of the party who would not have grasped at the slightest suspicion of an excuse to prolong the pilgrimage to the latest moment permitted by the social statute of

limitations. So, without being as thoroughly hila-
rious as other circumstances would have warranted,
it was still a merry party that boarded the *Ariel* to
return to Old Point.

" By the way," said Sid to me, as we left the
spires of Richmond in the distance, and had commenced the descent of the tortuous James, "now
that we are returning to the Roads, I don't mind
telling you that among the delightful surprises of
that never-to-be-forgotten night at Richmond, I
discovered my mermaid of Old Point. Dora says
that she first commenced to care for me at the
moment when, having become exhausted by the
buffetings of the surf, and having made up her
mind to become food for the fishes, I suddenly appeared like a messenger from Heaven knows where,
and cheated the aforesaid fishes out of their breakfast. But between you and me, my boy—but
breathe it not to ' Gath,' whisper it not in the streets
of Washington—between you and me, I've an idea
that the dear little thing wanted to scrape an acquaintance, you know, and so— Oh, you may
laugh, if you choose, and maybe I am a conceited
old humbug ; but you don't know what a way that
dear little woman has of carrying her points. How
do I know it was she ? If you had ever had her in
your arms once—which I presume you never will,

during the lifetime of the present incumbent, at least—you wouldn't ask so absurd a question. Why didn't she discover herself before? Now, see here, my boy, you are not as old as I am by several years, I believe ; but if you should hang around this mundane sphere as long as the late lamented Methuselah, you would never be able to penetrate the mysteries of a woman's motives."

Now we steam by the dismantled works at Drury's Bluff and turn into the famous Dutch Gap Canal, which, like many another of " Butler's follies," is a far-seeing example for wise men to profit by, and soon we are in the very midst of historic surroundings. Here is Harrison's Landing, where McClellan withdrew after Malvern Hill, and closed the Peninsular campaign by a disastrous retreat ; here is Fort Darling, and Bermuda Hundred, and City Point, and dreamy old Williamsburg, once the capital of the Old Dominion, the seat of a Catholic bishopric, and the home of a great university ; and here again is Jamestown, where naught but a tumbling ruin in a murky swamp marks the site of the first settlement on American soil. And thus we follow the sinuous windings of the James, along which the green fields are laden with a merry harvest, and hanging orchards are merry with the shouts of busy pickers and packers, and huge bluffs appear to impede and contest our progress, and shoal inlets and ambitious creeks make in and out, and dense forests come down to meet us, and distant hills mount and grow gray and white in the changing lights and shadows. Gliding, pushing, winding, rounding sharp points, coursing about swelling groves that come to the water's edge, steaming, puffing, whirling, and speeding with hot haste, we hurry into the broad mouth of the noble river, sweep around Newport News, and the whole magnificent breadth of Hampton Roads is before us.

Ah, the Roads! Like tired children returning to the love and protection of the benign mother, the weary, fainting pilgrims return to thee for comfort and repose. There is that peace and comfort in thy soothing presence that maketh glad the heart of thy children, weary and tired from delightful enjoyment. Tired of songs and laughter; tired of inglorious ease; weary of roaming, though never so enchantingly; weary of the sweet do-nothingness of life—glad, oh, so glad to return! Glad to return to the sight of thy boundless blue waters; to listen to their moans and entreaties; to follow them in their stately minuets or their merry. rollicking romps. Brave, matchless, incomparable old Roadstead, we salute thee!

*　　*　　*　　*　　*　　*

The general's dinner was perfect. It was not alone a banquet of solids and fluids—it was a feast of absurdity and a flow of downright imbecility. The superlative of *bonhomie* came in with the soup, and remained with the coffee. The salmon was washed down with liquid drollery, and the venison partaken to a *concetto* accompaniment, and sprinkled with the most saline of Attic salt. There were soft crabs and softer wit, oysters and optimism, boned-turkey and *bon-mots*, salads and ballads, following each other in bewildering confusion. We determined to eat, drink, and be merry, for to-morrow we expected to die to all intents and purposes. Then there were toasts and responses, of which the Scribe has preserved but one—and that his own—and for repeating which he craves plenary indulgence, pleading the irresistible temptation, for the hour was propitious, and the toast "Our Lady."

"Once upon a time," said he, "a fair mermaid, wandering from the court of Neptune, lost her way among the glittering aisles of the sea-caves, and, tempted hither and thither by glimpses of untold splendor, strayed from the sound of the Tritonic horns, and night overtook her, far, far away from the haunts where her merry sisters romped in bewitching play. Then, as bewailing her strange mishap, she darted here and there among the coral reefs and flowery beds, striving to discover some familiar mark to guide her weary footsteps to their home, she suddenly discerned the bright, twinkling stars shining through the deep, transparent waters, and deeming them the crystal lights from the halls of Oceanus, rose to the brink of the waters. There she found herself in the midst of a noble roadstead, where huge ships rode proudly at anchor, and the stern ramparts of strong castles uprose from the breakers, and the gray dawn was breaking through a rift of purple clouds on the edge of the far horizon.

"As she floated leisurely on the summit of the waves, wondering at the strange spectacle, and striving to comprehend the mystery of the heavens from which the twinkling stars were fading, she discerned not far away from her, beating against the surging waters, as if defying their buffetings, the figure of a fair-haired mortal.

"'What a strange being!' thought she. 'Can it be one of those unhappy creatures of whom the gods make merry sport; those wretched unfortunates whom we call the children of men? How fair he is!—how strong, how brave, how self-reliant! Can it be that such as he is denied the boon of immortality? What if I speak to him? What if I enchant and beckon him? What if I en-

tice him to our crystal halls, and lead him captive
in the train of our sisterhood?' Then she caught
sight of his clear, piercing eyes; his imploring, fas-
cinated gaze met hers; his valiant bearing and his
helplessness stirred her pulses, and her heart went
out to him. 'I will have compassion,' said she,
'compassion and pity and loving-kindness, and
thus may I fit him for a home among the immortals.'

"So, uttering a feeble cry, as of one in distress,
she drew him to her, suffered him to clasp her in
his arms, to bear her unresistingly to shore, and set
her feet on the shining sands. Then speeding from
his astonished gaze, she hurried to some mysterious
retreat, transformed herself to the form of a mortal,
enveloped her figure in pink garments, and took up
her mission. Thus has it come to be said among the
children of men, that 'Venus arose from the waters;'
thus did the benign goddess of love take upon
herself the burden of compassion and pity and
loving-kindness for man ; thus does she fit him for
a home among the immortals ; thus does she cheer
and gladden, encourage and make bright the pilgrimage of life."

Then did the pilgrims, with one consent, lift high
the sparkling glasses, and with the grim vision of
parting before them, with the dread fear that never

again would they stand together around the social board, but breathing a silent, hopeful prayer, drink the longest and happiest of lives to " Our Lady."

*   *   *   *   *   *

"By the way, boys," says Jack, as we lounge on the pavilion after dinner, " I am going to leave you to-morrow, you know, and I want to say that I am awfully sorry that this jolly old pilgrimage has come to an end. It has been the laziest, dreamiest, cosiest jaunt of all my life, and by Jove! I've enjoyed it. Sid, old boy, I am awfully obliged to you and Saul for not chaffing me too much over that silly little affair in the Dismal Swamp. I wonder what ever made me so desperately mashed over Dora? Of course you know she's the dearest little thing in all the world, and if I only had her for a sister I'd be ever so proud of her, and I presume I should love her to death. But then she didn't care a picayune for me, and besides, a fellow can't live on love, you know. There must be something besides to keep the pot a-boiling, on one side or the other, and when a poor devil like me thinks of settling down, he had better choose a brown-stone front than a cottage with roses. And, boys, now I'm leaving you I don't mind saying that I'm gone this time—head and heels—and I'm not ashamed of it either."

14

"Who's the lucky creature this time, Jack?" we inquire in concert.

"Who? Why, you know that magnificent brunette from Ohio, don't you? Miss Grosvenor. The one I danced with so much last evening—dressed in a dark blue silk, blue sash, blue gloves, and all that sort of thing. By Jove! she's a stunner, though, and they say she's worth a cool ten thousand a year. How's that? And I rather think she likes me—at least she said she was awfully fond of fellows with light hair and blue eyes and—and —and blonde moustaches," and Jack tenderly caresses the few downy sprouts that are beginning to spread timidly along his upper lip.

"But see here, Jack,'" says Sid, "if you haven't made any more progress than that I'm afraid you'll make a miss of it. Didn't I hear you say you were to leave to-morrow? You can't expect that your handsome countenance is already photographed on her heart, can you?"

"Now see here, Sid," responds Jack, with an air of injured innocence, "do you take me for a blamed fool? Don't you think I have been on the town long enough to know what I am up to? You know our paper was going to send a man to Ohio to report the campaign. Well, they sent a fellow who's got a mash in Washington, and he's written

to me, and wants to know what I'll take to exchange
with him. Was there ever anything more pat than
that—eh? So I've telegraphed him to go to Washington, and I'll leave for Cincinnati to-morrow morning. You see Miss Grosvenor is going home by the
morning train, and I've agreed to see her through.
What did you take me for, Sid? Did you ever
know me to stand back on a game when I didn't
hold any cards? But I'll see you all in the morning before we leave, of course. There goes the
Grosvenor all alone on the beach. I forgot to tell
her something about the train," and Jack disappeared on the trail of the blue silk.

"Jack is a right good fellow," says Dick, as we
watch him bowl along the sand, "but he's awfully
young and fresh, after all, don't you think so? I
can't understand how he had the insufferable im-
pertinence to propose to Dora. She's a splendid
little woman, of course, and I'd go through fire if
she asked me, but she'd be the last woman in the
world I would ever think of being in love with."
Here Sid and I exchange glances. "Then to think
of his aspiring to that grand composition in ultra-
marine! Why, she's as big as two of him, and, as
they promenade the beach out yonder, they remind
one of nothing so much as a lady with a yellow
poodle. But then we need never fear but Jack will

make his way in this world. If I had his cheek I would not mind proposing to the Queen of Sheba. But don't you know, boys, I feel wretchedly solemn over our breaking up. It has been such a glorious summer, you know; such a perfect symphony in neutrals."

"But you are not going to desert us, Dick?" says the Scribe with amazement.

"Well, you see the parting has got to come some time, and it's useless to prolong the agony. And, besides, my men want to know why I don't go to New York and start in with the campaign. I am billed for that town, you know, and, now Kelly and Tilden have locked horns, it looks as if a fellow might have his hands full keeping the run of things. So I've concluded to take the *Hopkins* to-morrow and swing round to Boston and see how the Butler canvass is booming."

"But how about the picture, Dick?" we inquire. "Have you abandoned the greatest effort of your life?"

"Now see here, boys, if you ever mention that picture business I'll never forgive you. Of course you know that was all an excuse to hang around Old Point, and get Dora to talk about painting and music and all that sort of thing. She's such a wonderful little woman, you see, any way, and she has

such a manner of making you think you know everything about anything, when, in fact, you don't know
anything at all. What a confounded fool she made
of me, by the way ! Why, after talking over that
ridiculous picture with her, I used to think that if
Turner or Correggio or Church or Bierstadt or any
of those chaps should happen around, I could give
them points in color and perspective that they
never dreamed of. But then I'm not sorry after
all. It has been such a delicious summer, and
boys, by the shades of Leonardo ! I don't expect
we'll ever see another like it. Just think of the
songs, and the water, and the jokes, and the sky,
and the green fields, and the stories, and the landscapes, and the rest. It has been a perfect *opera
bouffe* of blue and green."

And so the next morning we bade Jack a tearful
farewell as he departed for the Richmond train,
loaded with the bags and the bundles and the mis-
cellaneous luggage of the female Buckeye in blue,
and waved our handkerchiefs to Dick as the *Hopkins* backed slowly away from the wharf and turned
her head toward the Capes. Then leaving Sid to
bring up the goddess, I strolled off to our common
sitting-room at the hotel, where I found the general
buried behind the huge sheets of the Baltimore
American, and was soon lost myself in an effort to

catch up the dropped threads of the world's progress, of which we had been carelessly ignorant for
six long weeks. Soon the general throws down his
paper with a yawn, and turns to me.

"So," said he, "the poet and the artist have deserted us, and the disintegrating process has commenced. Do you know I haven't been contemplat-
ing anything of the sort at all? It has seemed as
though we were all to drift along together in this
vagrant sort of a style for the balance of our lives.
To be sure, nothing could be more absurd; but
then it has been a summer to be remembered. I
am a bluff old fellow at the best, and I don't care
for associates at all, and it is among the oddest
things in the world that I should ever have con-
sented to Dora's whim to loaf around the country
with a party of gentlemen of whom I knew nothing
except that they were exceptionally agreeable acquaintances; but you youngsters looked so deucedly
innocent, and lazy, and impudent, that your pilgrimage just happened to chime in with my mood,
and I went, and I should never have forgiven myself if I had not. I have enjoyed myself to the utmost, and, if I am any judge of appearances, it has
been the happiest summer of my little girl's life.
But the worst of it all is, it has come to an end.
Life is made up, my dear Scribe, of meetings and

partings; of the bitter and the sweet, and the bitter in undue proportion. This evening we will say 'Good-by,' and wish each other a prosperous future, and that will be the end of it. Perhaps we may meet again in the future, and probably we shall not, but I don't imagine we shall ever wholly forget this summer's pilgrimage."

Then the door opened, and to my amazement Sid appeared, smiling and confident, with our brave little goddess hanging lovingly on his arm. And what an astounding change had come over the whole presence of the Pharisee! Tall, slim, and athletic, he looked a very hero of romance, which his good forty years of contact with the world had polished rather than matured. The full, plentiful beard had been cleanly shaven from his face, leaving nothing but a huge blonde moustache that fairly swept to the tips of his big square shoulders, and disclosing a vivid scar that stretched from his ear to the swell of his lower jaw, the presence of which I alone among his intimates had ever known. With a courtly bow, as dignified and proud as that of a prince, he strode rapidly to the chair where lounged the gray old general, and detaching the hand of our clinging divinity from his arm, dropped gallantly on one knee before the astonished veteran.

"General," said he, "I am the most unworthy of

men. I haven't a single palliating virtue to offset a multitude of vices. I am a roving Bohemian, without home, friends, or country, and without a dollar to my name. I am, in fact, the last man of all the world to sue for the possession of its choicest treasure. But, general," and extending his hand, on which in glaring prominence shone a rare onyx ring engraved with the figure of a lion *couchant,* " I am come in all humility to demand the half of your kingdom."

" Thank God !" shouts the general, as he peers first into the face of the kneeling suitor, and again at the ring, which for the better part of fifty years had never left his person until that terrible night in the Wilderness. "Thank God ! at last ! Behold my son who was dead and is alive again— who was lost and is found !" and overcome by his emotions he opens his arms and throws himself bodily into those of the kneeling suppliant, as glad tears of joy course plentifully down his aged cheeks.

Then I glance at the pink figure of our dear little goddess. The large black eyes have been opening wider and wider, her abundant hair has been thrown back, and the graceful little figure bent forward to catch the slightest syllable ; and, as the great truth dawns upon her, and the two men clasp each other in a strong embrace, she utters one glad little cry, and kneels tearfully and hysterically by their side.

"Great heavens, papa !" she gasps ás she clasps the neck of the happy old soldier. "What *can* you mean ? Is it that my Sid is your hero of the Wilderness ? Yes, I can see it in your eyes. Why had I never suspected it before? As if it could have been otherwise !" Then proudly, as she threw one little white arm about either neck, "as if there could have been another in all the world as brave, as true, as noble as he !" And then, as her great love rose uppermost, "and, papa, do you hear ? He is all my own—all mine—*mine !* He loves me—your poor little Dora !—and he has loved me so long—and he would never have told me if I had not begged him to. O my poor, poor darling ! how you must have suffered for us. Papa, do you hear *him*—asking for your silly little girl—for *me ?* Why, it is all like a dream !"

"Darling," says the general, as he rises proudly to his feet, leaving the two foolish lovers still kneeling before him, "he has no need to ask from the two who are so proud of having anything to give. O my son !—doubly my son—and my daughter, don't you see that this is the proudest moment of my life ? May God in his infinite mercy guard and preserve you both."

Then, seeing that I am unnoticed and forgotten, I steal silently from the room, leaving them alone with their great happiness.

———

My dear indulgent reader, the pilgrimage is ended—the Scribe has no more whereof to scribble —though I can assure you from my heart that it is with sincere regret that I am

Finally yours,

Saul Wright.

PUBLISHED BY FORDS, HOWARD, & HULBERT,

27 Park Place, New York.

THE GREAT INDIAN NOVEL!

PLOUGHED UNDER:

THE STORY OF AN INDIAN CHIEF.

TOLD BY HIMSELF.

With a Spicy Introduction about Indians,

By INSHTA THEAMBA ("Bright Eyes," of the Poncas).

16mo, Cloth, with decorative cover design from Crawford's Statue of "The Indian." $1.

"Something unique in literature. . . . It will sustain much the same relation to pending questions of Indian Policy as ' Uncle Tom's Cabin ' sustained to slavery and anti-slavery agitation."—*Chicago Standard.*

" A story of the early impressions, experiences, and ideas of a young Indian chief, embodying many of the customs, usages, and legends of the red men, descriptions of hunts, battles, and incidents of many kinds, all interesting and all authentic. It presents their own notions of things, largely in their own words, and in the graphic guise of fiction makes known many significant facts, and depicts many characteristic fancies of theirs not familiar to the public."—*Providence* (R. I.) *Star.*

" The story is full of the interest of life, love, and adventure among these strange people, and contains much food for thought among our own intelligent and 'civilized' citizens. It gives a graphic picture of the Indian as he is—good and bad, like the rest of the world—and portrays the beauties of our ' Indian policy,' with its effect on the fortunes and its impression on the mind of a genuine red man. Such a showing of hidden facts is needed, and the public will welcome it, coming in such attractive form."—*New York Commercial Advertiser.*

" The writer has a keen sense of the satire of situations. . . . It is to be hoped that ' Ploughed Under' will follow fast in the footsteps of ' A Fool's Errand ' and ' Bricks without Straw.' It is as true of it as of them, that a mighty purpose to show up wrongs, backed by an array of facts and incidents drawn from actual life, has a tremendous force in opening people's eyes to truth, and making them think rightly."—*The Critic.*

PUBLISHED BY FORDS, HOWARD, & HULBERT,

27 Park Place, New York.

FIELD, FOREST, AND STREAM.

Flirtation Camp; or, The Rifle, Rod, and Gun in California. A Sporting Romance. By THEODORE S. VAN DYKE. 12mo, cloth, beveled, fancy gold-stamped cover, $1.50.

"A valuable addition to the literature of Sporting on the Pacific Coast, presented in the entertaining form of a story. Mr. Van Dyke is well known among the lovers of hunting and fishing, through his frequent contributions on those subjects to the best sporting papers; and his descriptions will be received as authentic. As a descriptive writer the author shows much ability, and the exciting incidents of the story, as well as the hunting exploits narrated, are vividly portrayed. Those who seek lower California for the restoration of health, or the pleasures of the field and stream, will find here many valuable suggestions."—*New York Star.*

There is a pleasant flavor of merry burlesque and humor pervading the whole tale, and the reader is alternately amused with his companions, charmed with the unaffected and graphic descriptions of scenery, intensely interested in the zeal of the chase, and instructed in the multifarious habits of game and arts of the sportsman. The story will be enjoyed rather by the lover of out-door life and adventure, than by the ordinary novel-reader. It is a wholesome, breezy, racy book.

Field, Cover, and Trap Shooting. By ADAM H. BOGARDUS (*Champion Wing Shot of the World*). 12mo, 443 pp. *Steel Portrait.* $2.

This admirable compendium of over forty years' experience is a complete book of its kind. It embraces hints for skilled marksmen, instructions for young sportsmen, haunts and habits of game-birds, flight and resorts of water-fowl, breeding and breaking of dogs, and other subjects of interest. Edited by CHARLES J. FOSTER, the veteran editor of the *N. Y. Sportsman*, it is in practical, available shape.

TALES OF THE BORDERS.

Camp and Cabin: Sketches of Life and Travel in the West. By R. W. RAYMOND. Little Classic style, red edges; with Frontispiece. $1.

"Dr. Raymond's ten years as United States Mining Commissioner gave him free range among peaks and canyons, valleys and 'slopes,' from the Rocky Mountains to the Pacific, and his keen eye and witty pen have made brilliant use of this opportunity."—*Cleveland* (O.) *Leader.*

"Mr. Raymond possesses a rare gift of lively description, and presenting the familiar talk of his characters with the racy unction of their local dialects."—*N. Y. Tribune.*

"Cannot fail to interest even a fastidious reader."—*N. Y. Times.*

Brave Hearts. An American Novel. *Illustrations* by Darley, Stephens, F. Beard, and Kendrick. 12mo, Cloth, $1.

"A successful experiment. It is a tale of two regions—alternations between the quiet scenes of New England and the rough, boisterous, and dangerous life of an extempore Californian."—*Philadelphia Evening Herald.*

"A really good American novel. . . . The purpose of the book is indicated by its title. It is a representation of *courage*, in various forms of individual character."—*Boston Globe.*

HARRIET BEECHER STOWE'S BOOKS.

DOMESTIC TALES.

My Wife and I; or, Harry Henderson's History. A Novel. *Illustrated.* 12mo, cloth, $1.50.

"Always bright, piquant, and entertaining, with an occasional touch of tenderness, strong because subtle, keen in sarcasm, full of womanly logic directed against unwomanly tendencies."—*Boston Journal.*

We and Our Neighbors: The Records of an Unfashionable Street. A Novel. *Illustrated.* 12mo, cloth, $1.50.

"Mrs. Stowe's style is picturesque, piquant, with just enough vivacity and vim to give the romance edge; and throughout there are delicious sketches of scenes, with bits of dry humor peculiar to her writings."—*Pittsburgh* (Pa.) *Commercial.*

Poganuc People: Their Loves and Lives. A Novel. *Illustrated.* 12mo, cloth, $1.50. (*Recent.*) In Mrs. Stowe's early inimitable style of New England scene and character.

"A fertile, ingenious, and rarely gifted writer of the purely American type, doing for the traditions of New England, and its salient social features, the same sort of service that Scott rendered to the Scotch and the history and scenery of his native land; that Dickens performed for London and its lights and shadows, its chronic abuses of every sort; the same service that Victor Hugo has done for Paris, in all its social state. Mrs. Stowe still keeps the field, and her harvests ever grow."
—*Titusville* (Pa.) *Herald.*

The New Housekeeper's Manual and Handy Cook-Book. A Guide to Economy and Enjoyment in Home Life. (Gives nearly 500 choice and well-tested receipts.) By CATHARINE E. BEECHER and HARRIET BEECHER STOWE. Nearly 600 pp., 8vo. *Handsomely Illustrated.* Cloth, $3.

"Considering the great variety of subjects over which it ranges, one is astonished to find, when he tests it by reference to any question on which he is personally well informed, how accurate is its teaching, and how trustworthy its authority."—*Independent.*

RELIGIOUS BOOKS.

Footsteps of the Master: Studies in the Life of Christ. With Illustrations and Illuminated Titles. 12mo. Choicely bound. Cloth, $1.50.

"A very sweet book of wholesome religious thought."—*Evening Post.*

"A congenial field for the exercise of her choice literary gifts and poetic tastes, her ripe religious experience, and her fervent Christian faith. A book of exceptional beauty and substantial worth."—*Congregationalist* (Boston).

Bible Heroines: Narrative Biographies of Prominent Hebrew Women in the Patriarchal, National, and Christian Eras. Imperial Octavo. Richly Illustrated in Oil Colors. Elegantly bound. Cloth, $2.75; cloth, gilt edges, $3.25.

"The fine penetration, quick insight, sympathetic nature, and glowing narrative, which have marked Mrs. Stowe's previous works, are found in these pages, and the whole work is one which readily captivates equally the cultivated and the religious fervent nature."—*Boston Commonwealth.*

PUBLISHED BY FORDS, HOWARD, & HULBERT,

27 Park Place, New York.

BIOGRAPHY AND HISTORY.

Life and Letters of John Howard Raymond, the Organizer
and First President of Vassar College. Edited by his Eldest
Daughter. 8vo, 744 pp. *Steel Portrait.* Cloth, beveled, $2.50.
" Dr. Raymond, whose simple life and stimulating letters are laid before us in
this volume, was one of the great educators of America."—*Christian Union.*
" Will be received with a peculiar interest by a wide circle of readers. . . .
Nothing can be finer than the enthusiasm with which Dr. Raymond entered upon
his work and afterward performed it. He will necessarily be remembered, and that,
too, with gratitude."—*N. Y. Tribune.*
"Not only a 'life worth living,' but a life worth reading about."—*Boston
Herald.*

Life and Times of Sir Philip Sidney. A Memorial of one
whose name is a Synonym for every Manly Virtue. *Illustrated,*
with 3 Steel Plates :—Portrait of Sidney ; View of Penshurst
Castle ; Fac-Simile of Sidney's Manuscript. 12mo. Cloth,
beveled, stamped in ink and gold with Sidney's Coat-of-
Arms, $1.50.
" Worthy of place as an English Classic."—*Pittsburgh Commercial.*
" There is scarcely any satisfactory memoir of him accessible to the general
reader, and the author of this book has done a good service."—*Phila. Enquirer.*
" Compels the reader's attention, and leaves upon his mind impressions more
distinct and lasting than the greatest historians are in the habit of making. . . .
We long to see the story of Sidney's life take its proper place in the hearts of American
youth."—*Christian Union.*

The Same. LARGE PAPER EDITION. Printed with red-line
marginal rule on large, heavy, cream-laid paper. Cloth,
beveled, with Sidney's Coat-of-Arms. Uncut edges, gilt top, $4.
" A book well deserving the beautiful printing and binding into which the Fords
have put it."—*N. Y. Evening Mail.*

Bismarck: His Authentic Biography. Giving many of his
Private Letters and Personal Memoranda. From the German
of J. G. HEZEKIEL. *Historical Introduction* by BAYARD TAYLOR,
late U. S. Minister to Germany. *Profusely Illustrated.* 8vo,
cloth, $3.50.
" Noteworthy for the fullness of its details and the great variety of hitherto
unknown facts and incidents that are recorded in it."—*N. Y. Sun.*
" If, as is alleged, 'history is biography with the brains knocked out,' this
portly volume may be appropriately called a chapter of *history with the brains
inserted,* for the history of Prince Bismarck is really the modern history of Germany,
and the key to that of modern Europe."—*Detroit Post.*

A Concise History of the American People. By Prof. JA-
COB HARRIS PATTON. *Illustrated* with Portraits, Maps, and
Charts; and containing Marginal Dates, Statistical Refer-
ences, and a full Analytical Index. 1018 pp., 8vo. Cloth,
beveled, gilt edges, $4 ; half russia, $6;

Reminiscences of an Idler. By the Chevalier HENRY WIKOFF.
Small 8vo, 604 pp. Extra cloth, beveled. *Steel Portrait.* $1.75.
" Has at once taken its place among the most racy of recent memoirs."—*Buffalo
Courier.*
" The charm of this book, which blends autobiography with reminiscences of
noted persons, and not a little rapid and interesting history, is that it . . . never
presents us with an anecdote or a reminiscence that is not interesting. The
'Chevalier' is never *dull.*"—*Hartford Times.*

PUBLISHED BY FORDS, HOWARD, & HULBERT,

27 Park Place, New York.

HOME HELPS.

The Easiest Way in Housekeeping and Cooking. Adapted to Home Use or School Study. By HELEN CAMPBELL, Superintendent of the Raleigh (N. C.) Cooking-School.

Compact with good sense, systematic, practical advice, well-classified and interesting information, and numerous Recipes chosen from the range of Northern and Southern Cookery, with hints from the housekeeping of foreign nations. *A book for families in moderate circumstances,* alike in town and country. 16mo, cloth, $1.

"Well planned and carefully written."—*N. Y. Evening Post.*

"It differs from other works of the sort in its brevity and in its attention to the preliminaries of housekeeping, which begin with the house itself, its ventilation, drainage, and water supply; . . . something about food before sitting down to eat it, and about the laws of health before health is gone."—*N. Y. Evening Mail.*

"All the directions are specific and clear, leaving nothing to chance. . . . One of the best cook-books for every-day use that we have seen."—*Troy* (N. Y.) *Budget.*

"Especially may we notice the chapter on sick-room cookery, and the thrifty and tasteful methods of utilizing fragments that would be otherwise wasted altogether. . . . New, sound, and practical—a trustworthy, compact, and thoroughly available guide."—*The American* (Philadelphia).

Maternity. A Popular Treatise for Wives and Mothers. *Seventh edition.* By TULLIO S. VERDI, A.M., M.D.

A monitor to young wives, a guide to young mothers, and an assistant to the family physician. Treating of the needs, dangers, and alleviations of the duties of maternity, and giving extended detailed instructions for the care and medical treatment of infants and children. 12mo, $2.

"A carefully written and very comprehensive work, whose author has for years been well known in Washington as an unusually able and successful practitioner. It treats of all the circumstances connected with maternity, under which the advice of a sympathetic and well-qualified physician is needed, with great ability. While the writer is clear and precise throughout, he is sensitively scrupulous in regard to the delicacy with which the subject-matter is approached and discussed. In addition to the strictly medical and surgical portions of the work, there are valuable chapters devoted to the physiological care and training of infancy and youth. In short, the whole contents will be at once recognized by any sensible woman as constituting a safe friend and guide."—*N. Y. Times.*

"One of the most interesting and instructive books of the kind that we have seen for some time."—*N. Y. Herald.*

"This book merits an extensive circulation."—*United States Medical and Surgical Journal* (Chicago).